LOVING AUNT LOU

Dating is dead for Lou Tonbridge since becoming sole guardian of her five nephews and their dog. Her city career on ice, she grapples with life in a warm, boisterous family. Then single dad Wes Drummond arrives in the village. The high-powered, corporate trouble-shooter finds that parenting his troubled teenage son is hard, yet not nearly as challenging as dealing with the attractive, but nutty, woman who keeps crashing into his life, his car, and finally his heart.

Please return / renew by date shown. M P
You can renew it at:
norlink.norfolk.gov.uk
or by telephone: 0344 800 8006
Please have your library card & PIN ready

RVS BALLS
29 -10- 19
Arot

19. MAR 14

14. APR 14

03. JUN 14

07 14

21. JUL 14

A27

A20
PS

M.

SARAH EVANS

LOVING AUNT LOU

Complete and Unabridged

LINFORD
Leicester

First published in Great Britain in 2008

First Linford Edition
published 2009

British Library CIP Data

Evans, Sarah.
  Loving Aunt Lou. - -
  (Linford romance library)
  1. Aunts- -Family relationships- -Fiction.
  2. Single fathers- -Fiction. 3. Love stories.
  4. Large type books.
  I. Title II. Series
  823.9′2–dc22

  ISBN 978–1–84782–944–3

Published by
F. A. Thorpe (Publishing)
Anstey, Leicestershire

Set by Words & Graphics Ltd.
Anstey, Leicestershire
Printed and bound in Great Britain by
T. J. International Ltd., Padstow, Cornwall

This book is printed on acid-free paper

1

'Hurry up!' said Lou Tonbridge, hustling her gang of nephews out of the house and into the watery sunshine. The chilly autumn morning was filled with the smells of damp leaves, sodden earth and wet dog.

Boys and dog piled into the bus while Lou slipped into the driver's seat. They were late again, which wasn't surprising. She'd overslept after being up most of the night nursing the youngest boy, Tom, who'd been sick into the wee small hours. Then she'd had to throw together breakfast while making school lunches with frozen bread.

She had forgotten to take the loaf out of the freezer the evening before and so had broken a nail as she'd tried to prise the solid slices apart.

Her brain felt numb and her eyes gritty. But that was the least of her worries. She had to get the rest of the boys to school.

The battered minibus took several goes to start. It coughed and wheezed, like an old man.

'Come on, baby, come on,' urged Lou, slapping her hand against the steering wheel that had once been smooth black but was now aged a crackled brown. 'You can do it.'

'Are we very late, Auntie Lou?' asked Toby who was sucking his thumb as if his life depended on it, staring intently ahead and willing the bus to go faster. He hated being the last one to arrive in the classroom and so far it had happened every day this week.

Lou glanced at him in the rear-view mirror. 'Not very,' she hedged, only just remembering not to cross her fingers because she knew he was watching for exactly that sign of weakness. Toby had his aunt totally pegged.

'But we are late?'

'Well, yes. But don't worry, sweetie, we'll get there before the bell.' As long as nothing else went wrong.

'I feel sick,' said Tom.

'Give him the bucket. Quick!' Thank goodness she'd had the foresight to bring one. The last thing she wanted or needed was the child throwing up all over the bus. Then they would be very, very late.

Lou sighed. Once she had been an organised businesswoman with a neat, compartmentalised life. Her days had run as smoothly as an ice-cold Pimms slipping down one's throat on a hot summer's day.

But since inheriting the boys, their mongrel dog, Ollie, an old farmhouse and, of course, the dratted bus, Lou's life had been a chaotic mess and one she never seemed to get the better of, regardless of what she did or how many lists she wrote.

The bus picked up speed as the engine warmed. A fine drizzle began to mist the windscreen. As they approached the school, it became steadily harder until the window wipers were straining to keep the vision clear.

A few minutes later, Lou pulled over by the other parked vehicles near to the front entrance of the high school, coming to a halt next to a very smart silver Porsche.

Luke and Dan bounced out, yelled goodbye and then bounced off across the wet playground.

Two down, two to go. As Lou hit the indicator and waited for a gap in the traffic, eight-year-old Caleb said in a gloomy voice, 'Luke's forgotten his lunch again.' He held up the offending tuck-box.

Lou squeezed shut her eyes for an agonised second. No! This would delay them further. She resolutely killed the engine and swivelled in her seat. 'Pass it over here, Caleb.'

It was only as Lou was belting across the playground in hot pursuit of her absent-minded nephew that she remembered she was still in her PJs and dressing gown and, ye gods, her bright pink fluffy slippers that the boys had bought specially for her. They'd been a surprise present a few days after they'd accidentally broken her favourite teapot.

Now who was being absent-minded, dashing about in her night attire?

Well, too bad about the get-up. There was no going back. And knowing teenagers, they probably wouldn't notice anyway. They were far too self-absorbed.

★ ★ ★

'Relax and stop worrying so much, Wes. Your son will be fine with us,' said Henry Scott, the school principal and old friend to the man restlessly pacing up and down the small office.

'I hope he will. It's time he settled down.' Wes Drummond didn't try to keep the exasperation out of his voice. He stared out of the window at the rain-slick playground. The few students braving the cold, damp weather were huddled in groups, hoods up, heads down.

He couldn't see Robin. He was probably sulking inside somewhere, determined not to like the place and hatching ways to make the teachers' lives hell so that they wouldn't like him very much either.

'He's been through a difficult period. You have to give him some leeway,' said Henry.

That went for the two of them, thought Wes. It had been a terrible time, what with the final torturous breakdown of his marriage after too many years of strife, having to sell the family home to pay Marina out, drastically changing his work commitments so that he could be home for Robin because, according to Marina, it was his turn to do the parenting thing. And, of course, learning how to be that parent after years of overseas travel.

He didn't really know how to be a dad and he hardly knew his son at all. Had he left it too late to salvage something positive?

It had been Henry's suggestion that

they move to Westerfield and Wes had reluctantly agreed, but only because he couldn't think of anywhere else to go.

His life was such a mess. He'd got to the point that he'd grab any lifeline that was thrown to him.

The bell rang for registration. Wes was just about to turn his back on the playground scene and to wind up his conversation with Henry, when his attention was snagged. There was a crazy woman, with wild tawny hair flowing out behind her, running helter-skelter across the tarmac.

She was wearing a man's blue and red checked dressing gown that flapped around her ankles, and revolting pink slippers. She skidded to a halt by one of the groups and handed over a box, tousled the recipient's hair and then ran back to wherever she had come from, dodging puddles and children alike.

Wes blinked, shrugged and then tuned into what Henry was saying.

'You'll see, he'll be happy here, Wes. As I've told you before, we have good staff and a fine school community. There's nothing to worry about. Robin will be making friends in no time. And as for you, you'll find Westerfield a soothing place to live after your difficult time with Marina and the divorce. Believe me.'

'Let's hope you're right,' said Wes. 'Because it's time we had a lucky break.'

A few minutes later, as he walked across the car park towards his Porsche, he heard a sickening crunch and screeching tear of metal. He hoped against hope that his car wasn't anywhere near the accident.

But of course it was. Now why wasn't he surprised? His run of bad luck just kept going on and on. He speeded up his pace and arrived on the scene just as a red minibus with more dents than a beaten bronze bowl was being reversed off the back bumper of his car.

And he wasn't terribly surprised that the bus was being driven by that crazy woman of the questionable dress sense.

'I'm awfully sorry,' she said as she wound down the window and offered a tight, nervous smile.

She looked pale and harried. There were dark smudges under her eyes that were either the result of the previous day's mascara or too little sleep. Her hair was the only vibrant thing about her.

'So you should be. That's my car you've just dinged,' said Wes trying to keep his tone calm, but hearing the tell-tale tension in it all the same.

'I'm pretty sure only slightly.' Her voice was melodic and low and mollifying, as if she was appeasing a three-year-old.

Wes didn't take kindly to being patronised. And especially not by a wacky woman in a Wee Willie Winkie outfit and clown hair.

'Slightly? How can you be sure? How about you get out of your bus and look just how much damage your reckless driving has done.'

It was obvious his deceptive mildness

didn't fool her for a second. He watched her eyes narrow and her mouth firm.

'But I can't,' she said. 'I'm already dreadfully late for the school run.'

'Dreadfully late?' echoed Toby around his thumb. 'But you said we weren't that late, Auntie Lou.'

'We weren't then but we are now, Toby. Especially if this gentleman insists that I have to get out and view the minimal damage I've accidentally caused to his precious car. Look, mister, can we work this out later? I do really need to drop the boys off at school.'

'Please, mister, I really need to get to school. I really don't want to be late again,' said Toby with heart wrenching pathos, as if being late for school was the worst thing that could happen to him in his young life.

'Well,' said Wes, debating what to say. 'I'm sorry, but — ' he didn't have time to finish.

'I'm gonna be sick again,' announced

Tom prosaically and retched into the bucket. Wes took an involuntary step backwards.

'Don't worry.' Lou tossed him a scornful look. 'He's over the worst. There's nothing left to throw up but bile.'

'I suppose that's a relief,' said Wes dubiously, wishing she hadn't chosen to share that piece of basic and unnecessary information with him.

'It is, believe me,' declared Lou with feeling. 'OK, sweetie,' she turned to rub little Tom's back. 'It'll be OK. Soon you'll be back home in your bed in no time.' She swung back to Wes. 'Look, I'll give you my details.'

She hastily searched for a pen. She found one, tried it out on the palm of her hand, shook it when it didn't work, tried it again then tossed it on the floor. She found another and that didn't work either. She scrabbled about in the glove compartment for a third one.

'Here, use mine,' he said and didn't bother to hide his exasperation. He handed her his sleek silver pen through the window and hoped none of the occupants were too contagious or anything. The last thing he needed was to get sick.

'Thanks.' She then began searching for something to write on.

'Now we're going to be dreadfully, dreadfully late,' said Toby in a voice of doom. 'My teacher will kill me.'

'No she won't. She's not allowed to,' said the ever-dogmatic Caleb. 'But she might give you lines.'

'What lions?' asked Toby his eyes widening in consternation.

'Shut up, Caleb, and Toby, stop being so melodramatic. We'll get there in time,' said Lou who then turned her attention back to Wes. 'Here, give me your hand.' She imperatively held out hers to Wes.

Wes frowned. 'Why?' But he held out his hand anyway, responding to her authoritative tone, and the next moment the impossible woman was scribbling on the back of it.

'Oi! What do you think you're doing!' he said trying to immediately withdraw it.

Lou held on to his hand for dear life. 'I haven't got time to mess about. Here's my phone number.'

'But — !'

'Ring me in about an hour and we'll swap details.' She then glanced in her rear view mirror, saw the coast was clear, put her foot down on the accelerator, careered into the road and belted off in a cloud of foul-smelling, black diesel fumes.

Wes stood there with his mouth open. Good grief. She was a total disaster. He looked down at the scribble on his hand. A wonky few numbers were sketched there. He raised his head again just as the bus disappeared around the corner, still puffing smoke. The woman was mad.

A brief inspection of his car showed a sizeable dent in the bumper. And he supposed, with the amount of dented bodywork in the bus, that crazy woman would think the damage slight. He shook his head. What a great start to his first day in Westerfield. If things didn't get any better, Henry has some explaining to do.

Wes drove back to the small cottage he'd purchased with his half of the marriage settlement. It was old and rundown and needed a whole heap of work expended on it. The real estate agent had said it had olde worlde charm. Henry had endorsed that description but with a big grin on his face.

For the life of him, Wes couldn't see the appeal. In his opinion, the only bit of charm it possessed was that it was affordable and close to the village so that Robin could walk to the bus stop and catch the coach to school along with the other village children. Other than that, it was just a place to eat, sleep and lick his wounds.

Inside, the cottage was as dismal. The low-beamed rooms were dark and oppressive and damp due to the central heating being in need of an upgrade. Unopened packing cartons littered the downstairs rooms. Last night they had taken out only the barest necessities to survive a couple of meals: the kettle, two mugs, two plates and the cutlery.

Wes now filled and plugged in the kettle for a coffee. He squinted down at the scrawled numbers on the back of his hand. He wouldn't call her, he decided. There'd be no point. She looked in a worse state than him. He'd be better off trying to find someone to fix the central heating so at least he and Robin would be warm.

It wouldn't help their black moods, but at least they'd be comfortable in their misery.

He scrubbed the telephone number off the back of his hand and then took his coffee into the small back room that he'd decided would be his study. His desk was already in place under the window. He sat in his black leather swivel chair and stared for a long moment out of the window at the untidy, neglected garden.

The garden was sad and desolate. Bare limbed trees dripped from the rain onto untended garden beds that should have been cleared weeks ago of dead summer growth. It desperately needed attention but Wes didn't have the heart to attack it and tidy it up. He didn't have the heart to do much except brood about his ex-wife's duplicity and how to fathom his moody, silent son.

Had he made the right choice to come here? Tucked away in a rural backwater to lick his wounds and piece back together his life? Well, he'd done it now. He was committed, at least for the near future.

With a sigh, he decided to write a list of the tradesmen he needed to kick-start work on the cottage. But in which box had he packed his office things? He spent the next frustrating half an hour opening cardboard boxes searching for a notebook.

2

'Was that someone at the door?' Lou asked, tossing an inquisitive glance over her shoulder. She was at the stove, stirring a huge pot of Bolognese sauce. Other saucepans of spaghetti and vegetables busily bubbled and steamed away. Outside it was sheeting down with rain. In the cosy kitchen the boys were good-naturedly squabbling over who was going to set the table for tea. It was hard to hear anything above the din, let alone a tentative door-knock.

'I said, is that someone knocking at the door!' she bellowed over the racket.

There was a lull in the argument. 'I'll go and see,' said Luke finally. He padded across the flagged kitchen in his rumpled grey school socks to the tongue-and-groove back door. He yanked it open. Wind and rain rushed in at the sudden invitation, causing Lou's carefully sorted pile of must-pay bills to scatter over the uneven stone floor and her rustic art gallery of the boys' paintings stuck on the wall to lift and flap as if they were a dozen seagulls following a plough.

'It's Rob,' said Luke. 'And he's soaked.'

Lou abandoned her cooking and came to the door. A boy of about Luke's age stood shivering in the dark, wet evening. His face was pale and his dark hair was stuck to his skin, reminding Lou of seaweed on the rocks after the tide had gone out.

'You'd best come in,' she said and peered out behind him, expecting an adult to be in tow. 'Are you on your own, Rob?'

'Yeah.'

Lou raised her brows in surprise. 'How did you get here then?' Of course, it was a stupid question because Lou could tell he had walked. He wasn't only wet with rain, but mud was caked on the lower half of his jeans and his joggers.

'I needed help with my homework,' he said, his eyes sliding away.

'Well, Rob, I've never known a boy so keen on doing his homework before,' said Lou. 'But you could've just rung Luke, you know. It's a terrible night for being out.'

'Our phone isn't working.'

'Ah.'

'Aaw, Auntie Lou, stop hassling him,' interrupted Luke.

'I wasn't, but you're right. No more talking until you're out of those wet things and have had a hot bath. We don't want you going down with a cold. Luke, take him up to the bathroom and give him some of your warmest clothes. Tea will be ready soon so don't hang about. I hope you like spag bol, Rob, because that's what's on the menu tonight.'

A few minutes later, they were all sitting around the scrubbed pine table with platefuls of steaming food in front of them.

'This is great,' said Rob around a

mouthful of spaghetti. 'Do you eat like this every night?'

'It's not always so 'licious as this,' said Toby solemnly. 'Sometimes we have spinach and sprouts and mashed swede.'

'Not all in one lump,' Lou laughingly protested. 'I'm not that cruel.'

'I haven't had a meal like this in ages,' said Rob wistfully. 'Dad can't cook.'

'What about your mum?' asked Lou, cocking her head on one side, interested to learn about this new strange friend of Luke's. His eyes and bearing reminded her of someone, but she couldn't think who it was for the moment.

'I don't see her anymore. She's gone to live in America.'

'Oh, I'm sorry. I shouldn't have pried.'

'It's OK. I'm sort of getting used to it.'

'Does your dad know you're here?' asked Lou, suddenly suspicious. She

20

hoped she wasn't aiding and abetting a runaway.

Rob shrugged and shovelled some more food in his mouth. 'He wasn't home when I left.'

'I'd better see if the phone has been fixed and give him a ring. He'll be out of his mind worrying if he turned up at home and you weren't there.'

'No, he won't. He won't have realised I've gone.'

Lou's heart went out to the boy. 'I'm sure that's not true. Now give me the number and I'll give him a call.'

She dialled the number and the phone rang out. Lou dragged a frustrated hand through her hair and then tried again. The same thing happened. She then rang the operator who told her the phone would be out of order for a while yet.

'It's no good, Rob. I can't get through to your dad so I'd better drop you home before he climbs up the walls with worry.'

She left Luke in charge of washing up

and teeth-cleaning and took Rob back to the village. The old windscreen wipers only just coped with the deluge. It wasn't a good night to be out.

At the cottage, the lights were on but his father was nowhere to be found. 'Perhaps he's out looking for you?'

'Shouldn't think so,' said Rob with a forced shrug. Lou itched to give him a hug, but refrained. She knew what teenage boys were like and she didn't want to embarrass him.

'Anyway, he's probably still at work.'

She was concerned about leaving him. 'Are you sure you'll be OK? I could stay for a little while until he gets home. Or we could ask your neighbour to come in.'

'I'll be fine, Auntie Lou,' he said, adopting the boys' term for her. 'Dad won't be far away. He doesn't work all night. Thanks very much for supper.'

'You're welcome anytime, but just tell your father first, OK.'

The minibus chugged through the wet night. Lou crouched low over the steering wheel, trying to see through the slashing rain. It was hard going. A mile from home, she swerved to avoid a massive puddle that had flooded part of the road, but she wasn't quick enough. The sheeted water flushed the under-side of the minibus, which then gave a splutter and cough and died.

'No, no, no,' she wailed. 'Not now. Not here. Not tonight!'

She was in the middle of the road, straddling the white lines. This was not a good place to be with the bus's headlights out. She fumbled in the dark to find the hazard lights, but she'd barely flicked them on when a high beam of light pierced the darkness right in front of her.

'Oh no!' she wailed again and shut her eyes, tensing against the anticipated impact.

But the other driver must have seen her at the last minute. He swerved, hit the same floodwaters she'd tried to avoid and ended in the opposite ditch, wheels spinning, motor revving.

Lou jumped out of the bus. The driving rain pummelled and drenched her in seconds. She ran over to the other vehicle. The nose was solidly in the ditch, the back wheels airborne.

Lou dragged open the driver's door. She grabbed hold of the person inside and tried desperately to haul him out, praying that the car wouldn't burst into flames and kill both of them. Through her manic, panicked struggles she realised he was addressing her.

'It would help if you undid the seatbelt.' The cold, hard voice clipped with anger was instantly recognisable.

'Omigod, it's you,' said Lou idiotically and let go of his arm. She took a step back and hopped from one foot to the other wondering what was going to happen next, apart from drowning in the storm.

Was he going to blast her? Throttle her for causing the accident? What?

The man switched off the engine and just sat there. The drumming rain and screaming wind were now the only sounds assaulting them.

'Er . . . are you OK?' Lou asked tentatively, shivering both from the saturation and cold as well as nervous tension.

'Not really.'

'Can you feel your legs? Can you wiggle your fingers and toes?'

'Is this some sort of *Simple Simon Says*?' he commented dryly.

'I'm just making sure you haven't broken your back or anything awful,' she said, stung. 'I could have just pinched you to see your reflexes instead of asking, you know.'

'Spare me.'

'But as you're obviously feeling OK, then perhaps you should get out of the car. Just in case it explodes.'

'I think we've gone beyond that possibility.' He released the seatbelt and unfolded himself with difficulty from the diagonally-leaning car, holding heavily on to the door to steady himself.

'Are you sure you're all right? I could

go for an ambulance. We're not that far from the nearest house.'

'A tow truck would be more useful. We can't abandon the vehicles like this. There could be another accident.' He shook his head and cranked his shoulders, wincing at the pain. 'What the hell were you playing at, parking in the middle of the road?'

'I was trying to avoid the flooded bit and then the engine died. It wasn't my fault.'

'But why didn't you have your lights on? I only saw you at the last minute.'

'My headlights died along with the engine. I was having difficulty finding the hazard switch. I haven't used it for a while.'

'You should have a permanent hazard light fitted to your head, lady!' he muttered.

'Excuse me?' She rammed her hands on her hips and glared at him.

'You heard.'

'I take exception to your prejudicial insinuations!'

'This is not the time for an argument.'

'I wasn't the one who started it!'

'You were parked in the middle of the damn road!'

'I'd broken down in the middle of the road. There's a difference.'

'Only a subtle one.'

'You are the most infuriating person I've ever met!'

He glowered at her evilly through the pelting rain. 'I could return the compliment.'

Lou stomped back to her bus and tried again to ignite the engine. It was as flat as a steamrollered dodo.

'We could try and push it off to the side,' she said gruffly as the man materialised alongside the bus.

'You have got to be joking. A bus this size is far too heavy to shift. We'd never succeed. And we'd give ourselves hernias in the process.'

He had a point.

Lou was momentarily disheartened and fed-up with the whole affair. She slumped low over her steering wheel, feeling wet, cold and miserable. She was also worried about the boys being at home alone. They could get quite boisterous just before bedtime, jumping on the beds and honing through the house and being as silly as puppies.

But there was nothing she could do about that so she'd best keep focused on the immediate problem.

'I'd rather risk a hernia than leave the bus here. So let's try and move it anyway,' she said with determined briskness, straightening her shoulders and raising her chin with purpose.

'Grief,' said the man but he got into position.

They strained against the bus, but their feet kept slipping and sliding in the wet and the ancient, dead-weight bus refused to budge.

Lou flicked wet hair out of her eyes and said, 'It's impossible. I'd best go and knock up the Kirks. They've got a farm just down the road. They'll be able to pull out your car and shunt mine to the side.'

'I'll go.'

'No, I shall. I know the way. It's not far.' She rummaged in the minibus and found one of the boys' plastic torches. The beam was low as the batteries were running out, but at least it was something.

'I'll come too.'

'No.' She shone the torch straight at him. It lit up his stark, beaky face and he winced at the sudden light. 'I think it would be better if you stayed with the vehicles in case help arrives.'

'Are you always this bossy?'

'Yes. It comes with the territory,' she said shortly.

She stomped off into the night, her beam of light getting weaker and weaker against the smothering blackness. She kept knocking the torch against her hand to make the beam briefly brighter and every time she knocked it, she thought of the aggravating man she'd left standing in the rain by the bus.

What was his problem? Did he think she had it in for him or something? It was simply coincidence that she'd pranged his car twice. Honestly, he was annoying. He only cared about his precious Porsche.

OK, so the Porsche was a beautiful car and if she had one, she'd be obsessive about it too. It wasn't every day you got to own a Porsche. It was heaps better than the old red bus.

And she had to admit, the Porsche suited the tall, sparse stranger. Both man and machine were sleek and dangerous, and wore the air of expensive luxury coupled with tensile power. Even the colour of the Porsche was coordinated to compliment the driver. The silver paintwork was similar to the man's short-cropped silver-blond hair.

The only jarring note was the man's antifreeze-blue eyes. They were disturbing in their intensity and always seemed to be full of anger.

After a few metres of trudging along the narrow road, Lou's torchlight faded completely. She ploughed on, but with slightly less confidence. Sure enough, the next moment, she slipped and landed in the same ditch that had claimed the Porsche. It was full of muddy, swirling, shock-cold water.

Great, thought Lou, stoically climbing out on to the road, now I'm really, really soaked instead of just being simply wet. She soldiered on, slopping into deep puddles and tripping over storm debris, until she finally made it to the farm.

*　*　*

The Kirks were brilliant. They brought along flashlights and a tractor and hauled both vehicles to safety.

While Josh Kirk fixed the chain to Wes's Porsche, he grinned at the scowling man.

'Nice car,' he said.

'It was until I met that nutty woman. She seems hell-bent on destroying it.'

'It was an accident,' Josh laughed. 'It could've happened to anyone on a night like this.'

Wes was disinclined to argue. He'd had enough for one day.

'We'll take your car to the farm tonight and then on to the garage first thing tomorrow, if you like,' said Josh. 'And I'll give you a lift home in a few minutes.'

'That's very good of you.' Wes hesitated, wondering about the young woman. 'What about the other driver? Will she be OK?'

'Lou? Don't fret about her. Mum's already taken her home. She was dead worried about those boys of hers. As for her old bus, I'll tow it away after I've done your car.'

'She'd be better off selling it for scrap,' muttered Wes. 'It's lethal.'

'Too right, but then how would she transport her boys around?'

'Boys?' Wes was curious in spite of himself.

'She's got five little 'uns.'

'Five?'

'She's a right battler, is Lou. She's doing a great job with those kids.'

'She's not married then?'

'Nah, and probably won't be with such a brood. Who in their right mind would take on a ready-made family with five kids, even with the lovely Lou thrown in for good measure?'

'Who indeed,' agreed Wes and then changed the subject. He didn't want to know anymore. The less he knew about this 'lovely Lou' the better. He didn't find her lovely. He found her totally unnerving.

Wes was dropped off at the cottage a while later. He immediately went into his son's room. Robin was asleep. Wes felt bad that he hadn't been there for Robin when he'd returned home from school, but the lunchtime meeting in the city had gone on far longer than he'd anticipated and then the weather had upset the running of the trains. The accident with that mad woman and her bus had been the final straw.

'I'm sorry, Robbie,' he said softly, touching the boy's dark, tousled hair. 'I never planned on you being a latch-key

33

kid. I promise I'll do better.'

The boy stirred. 'That you, Dad?'

'Yeah. Sorry I'm so late, son. I tried to get back in time but everything conspired against me.'

'S'alright.'

'Did you find enough food for supper?' Wes couldn't remember for the life of him what he'd left in the fridge. But whatever it was, it wouldn't have been very inspiring.

'I had tea at a friend's house.'

'Oh. A friend?' Wes had had no idea Robin had made any new friends. He hadn't said. 'What's his name, this new friend?'

'Luke Sommers.'

'I'd better call on his mum and thank her.'

'She said it was no sweat. I could go there whenever I wanted.'

'That was kind of her.'

'She's real cool.'

'Oh.' It wasn't like Robin to make such statements about his friends' mothers. 'How cool is cool?'

' 'Xtra special, super cool.' He yawned. 'Night, Dad.'

Extra special, super cool, eh? Wes grinned. He would have to meet this wonder woman who'd inspired his son's praise. She must be a great cook!

Wes left Robin's room and headed for the bathroom. He stripped off his sodden clothes and stood under the scalding hot shower.

At least the cottage's plumbing had been upgraded. He hadn't been a complete failure in that regard. It was good to let the hot needles of water pummel and massage his weary muscles. His neck was sore from the crash, but at least he hadn't received any worse damage.

As for his car, that was another matter. But he'd deal with that tomorrow when he wasn't so tired and grumpy.

★ ★ ★

After his shower, he went in search of food. He was ravenous. He had eaten

35

very little during the highly-charged luncheon meeting with his new clients and hadn't, unlike Robin, had the untold pleasure of a home-cooked meal this evening.

But he baulked as he stood on the threshold of the kitchen. It was an utter mess and not only because of the boxes of unpacked china and linen still cluttering the place. They'd been like that for two weeks now.

There were also dirty dishes in the sink and spills on the worktops. Wet washing was still locked in the new washing machine that the plumber had put in just three days ago.

Wes, not for the first time since his marriage had failed, felt defeated. But he knew he had to get his act together. If not for his sake, then for Robin's.

He purposely ignored the mess. Food was top priority.

He rifled in the fridge and found some hard bits of cheese, a couple of tomatoes and half a limp lettuce.

He took them out and cradled them

in his hands searching for a spare, clean plate, but everything was festering in the sink. He would have to tackle the washing up first after all.

He sighed and dumped the food on the breadboard. If he hadn't been so hungry, he wouldn't have bothered and gone straight to bed.

If they'd still lived in London, he would have rung up for a pizza.

If Marina hadn't left, she would have cooked one of her fancy dishes and the fridge would have been satisfactorily stocked with delicacies. Guaranteed, there wouldn't have been any hard cheese and dead lettuce.

Stop! Wes shut down on the 'ifs' because it didn't achieve anything but depression. He had to do the washing up anyway because if he didn't there wouldn't be any clean dishes for breakfast and the mornings were chaotic enough with the packed lunch routine without adding that to it too.

And his stomach would groan all night and probably keep him awake so that he would start listing and then sweating on all the things going wrong in his life.

Really, he wasn't coping very well and that irked Wes. It was crazy he'd let this get so bad. He was a trouble-shooter, for goodness sake.

Big corporations paid him massive amounts of money to overhaul their businesses and make them more efficient.

So why couldn't he do it on the domestic front? It couldn't be that difficult to have a tidy house, clean clothes and a hot meal on the table.

But it seemed it was beyond him.

Think about it logically, he admonished himself as he munched on his toasted cheese and tomato sandwich, sans soggy lettuce that he'd binned without any compunction.

What did he need and how could be achieve it?

Well, he needed a cleaner maybe once or twice a week. And maybe someone to lick his garden into shape.

As he was now working from home, he also needed to find someone with some basic secretarial skills to tidy up his reports and put them on disk.

So all he had to do was find the appropriate people willing to give him a few hours of their time. It sounded too easy. There had to be a catch.

He'd spotted an ad in the local parish magazine for a small employment agency. He'd ring it tomorrow and start getting his life into order. Hopefully.

* * *

'So let's get this straight, Mr Drummond,' said the briskly efficient woman on the other end of the phone. 'You want a secretary, a cleaner and a gardener. Is that correct?'

'Well, yes.'

'I think that can be arranged.'

'You do?'

'Leave it with me.'

'I shall, Mrs Bennett, I shall.' He tried not to sound too relieved, but it was like a huge weight was being lifted from his over-burdened shoulders. He'd explained to the agency owner that often he was away, though his business was based at home, and the woman had said she would happily be the go-between and supervise the staff.

'Sounds wonderful,' he said and meant it from the depths of his heart.

'I like to use local people,' Mrs Bennett had said. 'It's friendlier that way.'

'Ah. I'd find it better if they come when I'm out of the house.' He didn't want friendly. He wanted solitude. No way did he want some chatty cleaning lady distracting him from his work and telling him the ins and outs of village life.

'I fully understand.'

As soon as Wes rang off he left for London, his spirits higher than they had been for a long while.

Mrs Bennett, on the other hand, was immediately back on the phone.

'Lou,' she said without preamble. 'I have the perfect job for you . . . '

3

The next day Lou turned up with her mop and bucket and other cleaning paraphernalia. She wasn't taking any chances. A single dad and a teenage son didn't bode well for owning essential cleaning apparatus and Sally Bennett had told her the place was an absolute tip and in desperate need of a woman's touch.

Lou's touch, to be more specific.

'All the removalists' boxes are still stacked in every room after two whole weeks,' Sally had said. 'The Drummond men are living out of suitcases, for goodness sake, even though they both have perfectly adequate chest-of-drawers and wardrobes in their bedrooms. I know, because I checked. It's a scandal. The cottage is a dump. They need you to sort them out, Lou.'

Of course, Lou had recognised the

cottage as soon as she seen it. It was Rob's home. The lad was becoming a regular fixture at Lou's, but she didn't mind. He was no trouble and he only came when his dad was going to be late home from some business meeting or other.

Business meetings. Ah, she remembered when! Once they'd been part of the merry-go-round of her life. She'd been one of those power-suited women with a smart briefcase and shoes that had cost the amount she now spent on basic groceries for a week. People had hung on her every word when she'd delivered her reports. She'd been respected and important in her own small way.

But that was three years ago. Her life was on a different merry-go-round now. It involved odd dirty socks and scuffed shoes and torn trousers, endless meals and sticky kisses. Any reports that came her way were now school reports. And her lovely designer shoes and suits were packed away in the back of her old wardrobe, maybe never to see the light of a boardroom again.

Three years ago, before the awful accident that had claimed her sister and her husband and both sets of grandparents, Lou had employed her own cleaner and had had a secretary. She'd lived in a flat but if she had owned a house with a garden, then she probably would have hired a gardener too! She'd been a trendy, upwardly mobile, thoroughly modern woman with her own interior design business.

Hah! What a joke.

Because now here she was, cleaner, gardener and secretary, all rolled into one, to care for an unknown man whose house she was going to give a makeover if he wanted it or not.

Of course, when Sally had first told her about the three-jobs-in-one, Lou had protested.

'I know I'd mentioned it was time I earned some money,' she'd said half-laughing and half-exasperated. 'But not like this. I just thought I'd do a bit of casual work while Tom was at nursery. It would fit in with my lifestyle without putting too much strain on things at home.'

'But this job is perfect for you, dear,' said Sally. 'Once you get on top of it, the cottage will be a doddle to clean. You could do it in a twinkling. With your eyes shut.'

Lou gave a protesting snort. But she was tempted. She had to pay for the repairs on that wretched Porsche. The Porsche owner had apparently told Joe the village mechanic that he would pay for the work, but Lou had her pride.

'Come on, after keeping that huge rambling farmhouse of your spic and span, a tiny cottage would be as easy as falling off a log.'

'Maybe.'

'As for the garden. It'll be a synch. And you love gardening and this one is not a large one to maintain. It's a mere postage stamp. So you might as well do that too, while you're at it. You could do it with one hand tied behind your back, it's so straight forward and simple.'

'Why do I feel I'm being conned?'

'You're being suspicious for no reason, Lou, dear. But let me finish my pitch because I'm well into my stride now. So where was I? Oh yes, transcribing the reports. You're more than capable of doing the secretarial side of things and it can be done in your own time. Its just data that has to be keyed into the computer and put on disk for clients.'

'And don't tell me, I can do it with my eyes shut, with both hands tied behind my back while I fall off logs!'

Sally chuckled. 'Not quite. You might make too many mistakes and hurt yourself in the process! But you could do it once the boys were in bed. It will stretch and exercise that clever mind of yours and prepare you for greater things to come.'

'I already stretch my mind with algebra homework and there won't be any greater things for a long, long time,' said Lou mildly.

'My dear girl, you think that now, but those boys of yours will grow up faster than you'd credit. Just take my children. My baby is in her last year of university and my oldest daughter has two children. It won't be long before the grandkids will be doing algebra.'

'Point taken,' said Lou. 'Though I can't for the life of me imagine little Tom as a uni student. Or Luke as a responsible dad, come to that.'

So she'd let Sally persuade her and now here she was with three hours to work magic on the Drummond home. She put on a jazzy CD and then worked solidly from the kitchen outwards.

Sally hadn't lied. The place was a pigsty. It made her own home look like something out a slick Country Homes' feature.

She scrubbed the cupboards and then unpacked a couple of the kitchen boxes before tackling the living-room to make it live up to its name: a living area and not some tip for anything they didn't know what to do with.

Her three hours were up all too soon. There was still so much to clean and tidy, but it was time to collect Tom. Tired, but feeling pleased with her efforts, she vowed she would bring order to the Drummond household, if only for Rob's benefit.

That evening, Lou received a call from Rob's dad expressing his thanks for yet another night's hospitality.

'Mrs Sommers, Wes Drummond.' He'd called her Mrs Sommers since the first time he'd rung to thank her for having his son, and Lou hadn't bothered correcting him.

'Hi,' she said and rolled her eyes as soapy water trickled down her sleeve. She was in the middle of hair-wash night with the three smaller boys and she had shampoo up to her armpits thanks to all their slippery squirming as they tried to avoid getting soap in their eyes.

'I'm ringing to thank you yet again for having my son,' he said.

'It's no problem, really,' she said, trying to mop up the puddles forming around her feet while towelling dry Tom. 'I've told you before, Rob is welcome anytime. It's more the merrier around here. Now I really must go. I've got little ones in the bath.'

'I'm sorry to have disturbed you.'

'Don't worry. I'm used to it. Bye.'

After she put the phone down, Lou wondered if she should have told him that she was his new employee, but then decided that it wasn't relevant. And anyway, he'd find out soon enough. It was no big deal.

★ ★ ★

For a month she laboured indoors and outdoors at May Cottage. The pile of boxes diminished and order was being established. She felt a great deal of satisfaction in transforming the place from a warehouse and into a home.

Lou also prepared extra when doing dinner at home so that at least three nights of the week, Rob and his dad would have a decent meal. The notes left by her employer were almost pathetically grateful and Lou's tender heart went out to this man and boy struggling to come to terms with their new existence.

She remembered all too vividly how hard it had been for her adjusting to a completely alien life after the accident. There hadn't been much time to indulge in self-pitying grief, because she'd had to be there for the boys. But in the middle of the night, she'd lain numb under the bedclothes, not even being able to cry because she was too emotionally drained.

There had been no inkling of tragedy when her sister, Jan, and brother-in-law, Dean, had asked her to baby-sit the boys.

They had wanted to treat both sets of parents to a weekend away as a thank you for all their help with the children. Lou had been more than happy to pitch in. After all, it was only going to be for two nights . . . What could possibly go wrong?

The police had been on her doorstep early that Sunday morning. She couldn't remember too much about the following weeks. She'd just kept functioning while identifying the bodies, organising the funerals, winding up the estates on top of dealing with the boys' grief and their day-to-day needs because there hadn't been anyone else to help.

So she empathised with Rob and his dad and was more than happy to support them.

★　★　★

'Robin spends as little time at home as strictly necessary and when he is at home, he hides himself in his room with the door firmly closed and the music turned up so loud that the house shakes,' said Wes to Henry Scott one Monday morning.

They were in Henry's office and once again Wes was staring out at the playground. The sun was attempting to shine through the marbled grey clouds that hung low and heavy. Some of the boys were kicking a tennis ball about, using the basketball posts for the goal.

Henry shrugged. 'Give him time, Wes. It's no big deal.'

'But it's been a month. All I get out of him are monosyllables.' While he spoke, Wes watched Robin dribble the ball and then lose it at the first sign of an attack.

Henry tut-tutted. 'That's a typical teenager's form of communication. But he's doing OK in class. Gets his assignments in pretty much on time. He still isn't joining in with class discussions, but he's definitely growing in confidence.'

'I'm not so sure. I've tried to help him and talk to him, but he avoids me. I really don't think he likes me very much.'

Now Robin had the ball again only to lose it to some redheaded kid with fancy footwork.

'Wes, don't take that personally. Teenagers don't like adults, period.'

'Hah, that's where you're wrong. Robin does. He's got a crush on some older woman.' He winced as Robin missed a shot at the goal.

'Really?' Henry grinned, joining Wes at the window. 'Is he going to be a ladykiller like his dad?'

'Those carefree student says are long gone. Just like yours, old man. But I'm serious. He reckons she's super cool. Grief, Henry, just look at that boy play. He's got no idea.'

'Relax, Wes. Robin's doing OK. It's only a knock about before the bell goes. It's not FA stuff. Anyway, who is this super cool woman?'

'She's the mum of one of his friends. He goes around to their place after school. I've talked to her several times on the phone and she sounds very nice. I've also tried to meet her but she was in the shower when I called around and I didn't have time to wait for her.'

'What's her name?'

'Mrs Sommers.'

Henry frowned. 'Mrs Sommers? I can't think of a Mrs Sommers . . . Oh, of course! You mean — '

Wes hardly heard him. He was too busy groaning as Robin was tackled again by the redheaded boy and again lost the ball to him.

Wes shook his head. The boy needed some urgent father-son coaching. If only Robin would drop the emotional barriers and let him in.

Suddenly a woman ran into the midst of the budding footballers, halting the scratch game. Wes recognised her immediately. It was that wacky woman with the monster bus and bossy attitude whose sole aim in life was to destroy his car.

She headed straight for the red headed boy and handed him a lunchbox. She tousled his hair, just as she had done a few weeks ago. Just before she'd bingled his Porsche! And then she gave the boy a hug.

Next, she turned to speak to Robin

and then gave him a big hug too.

Wes sucked in his breath and stared in disbelief. That was his son she was cuddling in the middle of the playground. She had no right to do such a thing. She was a stranger. A crazy stranger with a dangerous penchant for destroying beautiful cars!

And then he was even more shocked, because it was quite obvious, even from this distance, that Robin was hugging her back.

'Who,' he said, aware his voice had crystallised into agate. 'Is that crazy woman?'

'What? Over with Robin?' Henry smiled and nudged Wes in the ribs. 'That, my friend, is Lou Tonbridge. If I didn't already have a beautiful wife and a pigeon pair of lovely kids, I'd be in hot pursuit of her myself, boys or no boys.'

'She's a walking disaster.'

'She's a gem. She's one of our warmest, friendliest and most cooperative parents on the PTA. The school would be lost without her. She's efficient, energetic and willing to pitch in to help or organise any fund raising scheme, however bizarre.'

'Spare me the list of her attributes. If anyone is bizarre it's her!'

'Lou?'

'And what's she doing manhandling my son? You tell me that!' Wes was already heading out the study door.

'But, Wes, that's — ' said Henry.

'On second thoughts, I'll go and ask her myself!' said Wes, not listening to Henry, and he strode purposefully down the corridor towards the front entrance.

4

Fury lent a terrifying swiftness to Wes as he bore down upon the unsuspecting woman walking across the parking lot.

Lou heard the rapid tattoo of footsteps and glanced over her shoulder. It took her only a split second to realise that the man homing in on her was as wild as a freshly bathed cat. His handsome face was rigid. His eyes sparked fire. He looked as though he meant business.

And that it was all with her!

Lou immediately went into defence mode. She stiffened her spine, narrowed her eyes and tilted her chin at a higher angle ready for the ensuing battle. Because she was sure there was going to be one. Wes didn't look as if he was just going to pass the time of day.

'I'm not anywhere near your precious

Porsche!' she declared, deciding to get in first.

'It's not my car I'm worried about,' he snapped. Red slashed his Nordic cheekbones and his antifreeze-blue eyes were laser-sharp. As for his voice, it was ice-cracking dangerous.

Lou took a step back, just in case things turned ugly.

'Well, I am relieved to hear that,' she said. 'It makes a pleasant change. I thought you were obsessed with that stupid car.' She took another step backwards.

Perhaps she shouldn't have mentioned that last bit about the Porsche being stupid. What had possessed her? A death wish?

'What were you doing with my son?'

'Your son?'

'In the playground. You were manhandling the boys.'

'Correction, I was hugging — not manhandling — my nephew and his friend.'

'Precisely.'

There was an ominous beat of silence as Lou processed what he'd just said. And went cold.

'Omigod! You mean Rob's your son?' Lou shivered as a nervous sweat broke out all over her body, from the top of her head to the tips of her toes. Why hadn't she guessed?

She'd known Rob had reminded her of someone. Why hadn't she realised who it was?

And then another nasty realisation took hold. That meant that this man was Wes Drummond. Which meant he was her new boss.

Which meant that he was paying her so that she could pay for his wretched Porsche repairs.

Which also meant that she couldn't let him find out who she was because she needed to earn enough cash to pay the mechanic. Goodness, tangled webs had nothing on it.

'I don't want you anywhere near my son!' Wes snarled at her. 'You're totally unstable and dangerous.'

That was unfair! Lou riled up in self-righteous indignation. 'How dare you! I'm no more unstable and dangerous than you are.'

Though the way he was acting, Lou thought she'd maybe got that wrong. He was definitely showing signs of dangerous instability. But she wasn't going to point that out to him in a hurry. He was already mad enough.

And as he was her very-necessary-employer she was duty bound to keep her temper dampened down. She didn't want to blow everything and end up without a job because then she'd really be in trouble and wouldn't be able to pay a penny for the Porsche's panel beating.

Thank goodness Wes had never been at home on her May Cottage cleaning and gardening days. And thank goodness he only knew her professionally (if a cleaner-cum-gardener-cum-typist-cum-occasional-cook was deemed professional), as Louisa.

Hopefully he wouldn't make the

connection anytime too soon that Louisa was Lou-the-Porsche-Slayer-and-Son-Hugger.

Wes now had his hands on his hips and feet splayed in an aggressive, macho you-do-as-I-say pose. 'Keep away from my son! Do you hear me?'

Lou snapped shut her mouth. However much she wanted to retaliate and tell Mr Wes High-and-Mighty Drummond what she thought of him, it wouldn't do.

Not only did she want to keep her job, but she also owed it to Rob. That poor boy needed the haven of her little family and she didn't want to jeopardise anything by telling Wes Drummond exactly what she thought of him and his parenting skills.

'I demand that you have nothing more to do with him! Promise me!'

Lou continued to keep silent. She wasn't going to make any rash promises that she couldn't keep.

If Rob turned up on her doorstep, she wouldn't send him away. At least not straight away. She'd feed and mother him first.

'Have you got that?'

She briefly unclamped her lips. 'Yes. I heard you loud and clear,' and then she squeezed them together again because she was in danger of saying so much more to this uptight, arrogant man.

Such as explaining that it was Rob who had sought her family out, not the other way around.

And that she was only trying to provide a little domestic comfort for the boy because he clearly wasn't getting it from home.

And that she wasn't in the habit of hugging all and sundry, only those she cared about.

'No more contact,' Wes barked. 'At all.'

Lou almost saluted but refrained. She mustn't antagonise him further.

'I'll be watching you!'

'Have you quite finished?' she said. 'Some of us have more important things to do than yell at people.'

Like finishing the school run. Lou still had the three younger ones waiting in the bus and Toby would never forgive her if they were late again.

'I wasn't yelling.'

'Near as.'

'Just remember,' he said through gritted teeth, ignoring her comment. 'That I'll have the authorities on to you if I catch you within three feet of Robin.'

Lou kept a desperate hold on her temper. It was boiling up inside of her like a cauldron full of bubbling pea soup on an open fire. If he continued to provoke her, it was in danger of spilling right over and then it would be Lou who'd be doing all the yelling.

She counted to ten while inside she seethed. Just what did Wes Drummond take her for? Did he think she was leading Rob astray? The man was deranged. No wonder his wife had left him.

In fact, she was amazed he'd ever found anyone to marry him in the first place!

She reached ten but didn't trust herself to speak civilly so she simply turned on her heel and headed for the bus.

* * *

After delivering the boys to school, Lou drove home and wasted little time in ringing Sally Bennett at the employment agency.

'Whatever you do, Sally, do not let on to Wes Drummond that I'm his employee,' she said.

'Why on earth not? He's a lovely man, which you'll soon discover when you finally meet him. You'll get on like a house on fire. I can feel it in my match-making bones.'

'If any fire is involved it will be quenched on contact,' said Lou. She then added, 'Or end up being an inferno. Believe me.'

'Oh, Lou dear! How delicious. Do tell me more.'

'No. It's too complicated to explain.

But I really, really need you to keep my identity secret, at least for the time being. I don't want that bigoted jerk, Wes Drummond, to know who I am until I've made enough cash.'

'Bigoted jerk? Hmm. This is sounding more intriguing by the second. And judging by your tone am I right in thinking you've already met him?'

'Yes, several times.' Lou sighed. 'But he doesn't realise that the woman who makes him spitting mad is the same woman who washes his socks and holds his body and soul together with good food and nurture on the home front.'

Sally gave a delighted crow of laughter. 'My dear Lou, it sounds like love. You may have finally met your match.'

'No. Definitely not!'

'The woman doth protest too much,' said Sally and she chuckled some more.

'It's not a laughing matter,' said Lou sourly. 'Love and Wes Drummond do not go hand in hand. He would rather have me strung up and hung, drawn and quartered with a blunt spoon rather than love me.'

'You haven't told me what you need the money for? Is it something special? A holiday? A new car?'

Lou squirmed. 'I'd rather not say.'

'Tell me.'

'The repairs on Wes Drummond's Porsche.'

There was a startled silence, then Sally's voice breathed down the phone. 'Oh Lou!'

Lou closed her eyes and shuddered. 'Precisely.'

'I saw the car in Joe's workshop.' Sally paused. 'It was having an extensive makeover and Joe was rubbing his hands in glee.' There was another meaningful pause. 'So you caused those dents in the bodywork.'

'And the bumper,' Lou groaned. 'Why couldn't he have had some cheap car rather than a luxury, top-of-the-range model?'

'Because he's a top-of-the-range sort of guy, you must admit.'

'That makes me feel heaps better! Why did I have to tangle with him of all people?'

'Oh Lou,' Sally breathed again but with a catch in her voice. The next moment peals of laughter rolled down the line.

Lou glared at the receiver. 'I thought you were my friend,' she said once the laughing had turned to unladylike hiccoughing.

'I am. I am. Mum's the word. I promise I won't tell Drummond-the-Dish that you're his nemesis, however tempting.'

'Thank you,' she said dryly. 'And now for one other favour. Can you baby-sit tonight? I have a PTA meeting.'

★ ★ ★

Lou was late for the meeting. She was always late. There never seemed to be enough minutes in the day for her to achieve all the things on her must-do list.

She drove as fast as she dared along the winding road to the school, trying to brush the tangles out of her hair as she went. Where had the last couple of hours gone?

She'd thought she'd had everything in hand. She'd cooked an easy tea of baked beans and poached eggs on toast, had the three younger children bathed and in pyjamas and had supervised the homework of the older ones.

She'd left strict instructions for Luke and Dan to have their showers, have half an hour of television or computer games, and then go to bed early. Even Sally had turned up on the dot of seven.

Everything had gone smoothly until Lou had opened the back door to leave. As she'd stepped outside into the chilly night she was accosted by an evil-smelling, mud-encrusted Ollie.

Dan had left him outside after feeding him and so Ollie had ecstatically greeted Lou as if he hadn't seen her for a week. He jumped up and dirty paws hit Lou's clean, pale blue fleece smack on the chest and then they'd scratched down her clean jeans, leaving tramlines of mud.

'Oh you wretched dog,' she'd cried, pushing the offending beast off her. She yelled for Dan to wipe Ollie's paws and coat as she ran back inside the house and upstairs to change. She'd only had a not-quite-so-clean purple fleece and definitely not-very-clean jeans to replace the dog-destroyed ones. Tough, it would have to do. At least it was only the PTA. There was no-one there who she needed to impress.

And now here she was, rattling to the meeting and already ten minutes late. She threw the bus into the nearest vacant parking space and legged it into the school. The meeting was always held in the school library on the first floor. She ran up the stairs two at a time and then burst through the double doors in a rush, plonking herself down in the nearest chair.

'Sorry I'm late, everyone,' she said

with a general, apologetic smile.

'Glad you could come at all,' said Henry, good-naturedly.

Lou dragged out her notebook and the minutes of the previous meeting from her duffel coat pocket and then took stock of who was there.

It was the usual crowd. Henry and a few keen teachers, the regular handful of stalwart, helpful parents, and then those others that liked to be seen and heard but not coerced into jobs.

But there was one extra person tonight and Lou got a nasty shock. Her breath stopped mid-throat and her heart began to hammer hard. Pow! Pow! Pow! So that she was sure everybody in the room could hear it.

Because that extra person was Wes Drummond.

'I don't know if you've met our new parent, Lou,' said Henry with suspicious blandness. 'I've just been introducing Wes Drummond to everyone.'

'We've already met, thanks, Henry,' said Lou tightly.

'Ah, that's right. Your two boys are good friends.'

Wes didn't exactly scowl but his face tautened and his eyes froze to arctic-sea blue.

'Yes, Rob's a nice lad,' said Lou, holding Wes' icy stare with one of her own. Was it just her imagination or had someone turned the heating off, because it felt as if the room temperature had plummeted to well below zero.

'Now, down to business,' said Henry. 'Bonfire night will soon be upon us and the school is meant to be running the hotdog and soup stall again on the village green. We need a volunteer to organise it.'

He smiled expectantly at Lou.

'Sorry? What?' said Lou. She wasn't paying attention. Wes Drummond had thrown her concentration. She shivered and dragged her focus back to Henry. 'You were saying?'

'A volunteer. Bonfire night. For the hotdog and soup stall . . . ' offered Henry helpfully.

'You did it so well last year,' said one of the mums who'd never helped with anything except dobbing people in for jobs she had no expectation of doing herself.

'I second that,' said the woman's friend who also never did anything to assist.

'Er, we didn't actually have a motion to second,' said Henry. 'Lou?'

Lou was glowering down at her minutes. That Wes Drummond really got her goat. Why did he have to be here? He wasn't going to start popping up like some bad penny at all the school and village functions, was he? If he did, her identity might be rumbled sooner rather than later.

'Lou, what do you say? Would you like to organise it again? Especially as you know what you're doing,' urged Henry.

'If no-one else wants to,' she said without enthusiasm, still too preoccupied with Wes's unexpected presence to put up any sort of fight.

There was a collective sigh of relief.

'Can I second the motion now?' said the woman's friend.

The meeting ground on and Lou ended up with an impressive list of things she had to follow up, as per usual.

She smothered a yawn and took a sneak peek at her watch. She hoped Luke and Dan were in bed and that Sally wasn't being conned into playing endless card-games with them.

She then took a surreptitious peek at Wes Drummond. He was sitting there impassively listening to Henry winding up the meeting. He hadn't volunteered very much during the evening. In fact, he'd volunteered for nothing at all.

She wondered why he'd bothered coming. He'd have been better employed spending the evening with Rob and doing some important father-son bonding.

She took careful stock of him. It was the first time she'd really had a chance to study the man who was fast becoming the bane of her life.

He wasn't bad to look at. Not bad at all. She already knew he had a tall, spare frame but she hadn't been able to get a really good look at his face in repose. Before, it had always been contorted with anger or dripping with rain. Or both.

It was a surprisingly pleasant face — angular with hard planes and a decisive nose and chin. His silver-blond hair was cropped short in a no-nonsense style. If it were a smidgen longer, it would soften the patrician haughtiness and make him almost human.

As for his eyes, she knew how ice-cold they were. They reminded her of frozen Northern seas. Of course, she couldn't see his eyes for the moment because he was jotting something down in a small black notebook and the sweep of his long dark lashes hid the blueness.

Tonight he was wearing a muted-brown tweed jacket with leather patches on the elbows. It looked old and worn as if it was an old favourite. Like her, he was in jeans, but his were black and pressed to within an inch of their life. She knew, because she had ironed them just a couple of days ago.

He was in good shape and actually, she had to admit, rather sexy. It was a shame his personality didn't match his body. But then it would have been criminal for him to score high in both looks and personality. Westerfield wouldn't have been ready for it. And she definitely wasn't.

She smothered a smile as her glance slid back to his face and then was frozen by a sudden blast of arctic frost, because Wes was regarding her as intently as she'd been regarding him.

She immediately dropped her eyes but the damage was done. He'd caught her staring. Drat. She didn't want him to think she was interested or anything.

For a minute or two she kept her eyes lowered and concentrated on picking off what looked like dried porridge that was stuck to her jeans.

She then braved another glance and

realised his eyes were now roaming over her. She knew she looked dishevelled and grubby and cursed Ollie for his exuberant doggy boisterousness.

If ever she'd needed a boost to her morale by looking good, it was now. And it wasn't going to happen.

She always seemed to be at a disadvantage in Wes Drummond's presence. No wonder he thought she was a fruitcake.

* * *

Lou slipped away from the meeting as soon as Henry announced it closed. As she clattered down the stairs she heard footsteps behind her.

'Wait!' someone's shout echoed down the stairwell.

Lou sighed in defeat. The PTA mafia had caught her. No doubt to add extra fund raising duties to her already long list.

She turned on the landing near the art room door. 'Yes?' she said and then sucked in a surprised breath. The person calling her was Wes Drummond. He was the last person she expected. 'Mr Drummond?'

She waited until he'd caught up with her and then braced herself for the attack that was surely going to come, shoving her hands on her hips, getting into aggressive mode.

'I can't think that you have anything more you want to say to me. Unless of course you want to volunteer for the hotdog stand?'

'It was about my car.'

'What? The precious Porsche?'

She inwardly smiled when Wes' eyes narrowed at her sarcastic tone. He then glanced upwards towards the library.

The other parents and teachers were beginning to come down the stairs.

'Let's go in here.' He gestured to the art room and already had his hand on the doorknob when Lou squeaked a protest. Her heart was suddenly pounding. The last thing she wanted to do was be hustled into the dark, shadowy room with him. Anything could happen!

'OK, then I'll walk you out to your bus,' he said.

'No need. I can find it on my own, thank you,' said Lou, feeling niggled at his high-handedness.

'I'm sure you can, but I want to talk to you in private and not with the PTA breathing down our necks.'

He took her arm in a firm grip and began half guiding her, half dragging her down the stairs. It was a relief when he released her as soon as they were in the parking lot.

'Joe tells me that you've insisted on paying for the repairs.'

'Of course. I told you I would. You may take me for a complete flake, but I do honour my responsibilities.'

'I'm adequately covered by insurance. You don't have to bother.'

'Bothering doesn't come into it. It's the least I can do. I caused the damage, I pay for the repairs.'

'I won't accept the money.'

'I'm not paying it to you.'

'Joe won't accept the money.'

'He will.'

'He won't.'

'He will. I'm a valued customer.'

Wes gave a short, hard laugh. 'I'll be a more valued customer. One component of my car would pay for your whole bus.'

'Joe enjoys working on my bus. It's a vintage model.'

'I bet you he prefers working on my Porsche.'

'Why? Just because it's flashier doesn't mean it's better.'

'This is ridiculous. Why do I always end up arguing with you?'

'It's not my fault!'

'There you go again. Stop! You are one ornery woman. Just leave the bill paying to me, OK?'

'Fine. See if I care.'

There was a cough behind them and Lou turned around.

'Yes?' she said much more tartly than usual.

'So sorry to interrupt,' said the man.

He was one of the parents from the meeting. 'But I just wondered if you could organise . . . ' He rambled on about the Christmas fayre that was to be held in the school hall in a few weeks time and he was keen to off-load some of the admin work.

'Will you do it, Lou?' he asked.

'Yes, yes, of course,' said Lou who didn't want to do it in the slightest. But she was too distracted with Wes Drummond to object.

'Why do you let them do that to you?' demanded Wes in ill-concealed exasperation as the man trotted away wearing a smug smile of a job well hand-balled.

'What's bugging you now? He wasn't asking you to do anything.'

'That PTA lot,' and he waved towards the school building, 'just use you. You accepted every job that was thrown at you. Don't you have any backbone or do you like being walked over?'

'That's enough!' Lou held up her

finger as if admonishing one of her boys or Ollie the dog. 'I choose to help on the PTA. I have a duty to support my boys' school. And as for being walked over, no, I don't like it, which is why I don't like you trying to browbeat me. Good night, Mr Drummond.'

Lou got in her bus and roared away, once again leaving Wes in a cloud of black pungent smoke.

She was ornery? She liked that. He should take a good look in the mirror sometime. He'd be in for a nasty shock.

And as for being walked over . . . It made her blood boil just thinking about it. She was no wimp. She'd proved that over and over again these past three years.

She'd like to see how he'd react having to sell a precious business and take on five boys without any prior experience.

She'd like to see him learn how to put on nappies, toilet train a toddler, cook vast meals and cope with boys' bedwetting.

She'd like to see how he would handle the bone-numbing grief of five little boys while she also grappled with her own grief and its fallout.

She'd like to see him . . .

. . . grovel on his knees and say sorry and that he'd got it all wrong. That she wasn't a flake.

That she wasn't a wimp but a capable, strong woman who was in charge of her own destiny (and five boys, a dog and a dodgy bus).

But why, said a little niggling voice. Why did his opinion matter?

Lou didn't have the answer to that one. Well, not one that she wanted to acknowledge.

So she resolutely ignored the little voice and tried to put Wes Drummond out of her mind.

But that was easier said than done and the infuriating man dominated her thoughts for the entire drive home.

★ ★ ★

81

Once back at the farm, Lou parked the bus in the barn and made her way into the quiet house. Sally met her at the door.

'All OK on the home front?' Lou asked with a tired smile as she flopped herself in the nearest easy chair and eased off her joggers.

'Yes, but we do have a visitor. Robin Drummond. He's asleep on the couch.'

Lou shut her eyes in despair. She could picture it now — the police turning up with social workers and taking her boys off her and all because she'd felt compassion for a teenage boy trying to make sense of his parents' divorce.

'He was going to walk home, but I didn't like the idea of him trekking alone in the dark.'

'I usually drop him home,' admitted Lou on a sigh.

'I gather he comes here often.'

'Four or five times a week.'

'And what does Wes think of that? I only ask because of your interesting relationship with him.' Sally's eyes twinkled.

'That's a diplomatic way of putting it,' Lou laughed and then she became serious. 'Wes doesn't want me anywhere near Robin. He's threatened the authorities if I ignore his wishes.'

'But why, for goodness' sake?' said Sally, appalled. 'You wouldn't hurt a fly.'

'He reckons I'm a flake. But he should try running a household with five boys and a scatty dog. It can make the sanest person fray at the edges.'

'You're right. He needs his head examined. He obviously doesn't understand you at all. But don't worry about it now. I'll drop Robin off on my way home. There's no point you turning out again. You look exhausted.'

'Thank you, Sally. I owe you. But you'd best not hang around. Wes will be wondering where Rob is. Wes was at the PTA tonight, which is why Robin probably decided to come over. He usually pops around here if he's left alone at the cottage.' Lou groaned. 'Wes is probably doing his nut.'

'Oh dear. I suppose so, especially as he doesn't want Robin here.'

'Actually, I'm not sure if he's realised that Rob's trips to the farm are connected to me.'

'But you said he'd banned Robin from coming here.'

'No, he's banned me from seeing Robin. That's a completely different thing. He hasn't banned him from coming here.'

'I don't understand.'

'He thinks I'm two different women.'

'Come again?'

'When Rob comes here, Wes thinks he's coming to the home of Mrs Sommers. When he sees me in the village, he knows me as Lou Tonbridge.'

'I'm confused.'

'Well, Sommers is the boys' surname. When Wes first rang me he made the quite logical assumption that I was Mrs Sommers. I was pre-occupied at the time and so I didn't bother to correct him. I'd no idea it would become an issue. And then as things grew more awkward, I realised I'd missed the opportunity to set the record straight.'

'Oh, Lou.'

'Life's grown very complicated since Wes Drummond walked into it,' said Lou ruefully. 'There's never a dull moment.'

5

Henry offered to give Wes a lift home after the PTA meeting but Wes declined. 'I'm OK. The walk will do me good,' he said.

'Don't be daft. It's trying to rain again and I drive just about past your doorstep. Anyway, I have an ulterior motive. You can help me lock up the school.'

'Fine. I don't mind doing that but I'm still walking home.'

'But I've got another motive. My wife is out at a church meeting, so I thought I'd come in and have a sneaky nightcap.'

'It's drinks at my place then,' said Wes with a grin. 'But I'll tell you now, if this is a ruse to coerce me onto the PTA, it won't work. I've seen first hand how that committee works and it's not for me. You can't bully me into things like you do that Tonbridge woman.'

'Lou's a honey,' declared Henry. 'With her on the PTA, my life runs smoothly.'

Wes declined to say anything but it was his personal opinion that a smooth life and Lou did not go hand in hand.

★　★　★

When they arrived at May Cottage, it was in darkness. Wes switched on the lights and prepared the drinks.

'I had my doubts, but this place is beginning to look like a home,' said Henry settling himself into one of Wes's squishy leather armchairs and giving an approving look around.

'Not because of my efforts,' admitted Wes, handing him a brandy. 'It's my amazing cleaner. She's done miracles in such a short space of time.'

'Who is she?'

'Louisa somebody-or-other. I got her through Sally Bennett's agency. She's worth her weight.'

'Louisa?' Henry frowned. 'I don't know any Louisa's in the village. Maybe I should ask Sally about her. My wife is always going on about the drudge of housework. She'd love to have a cleaner.'

'You're not pinching my cleaning lady, you old rogue,' laughed Wes. 'I'll fight you for her.'

'Mops at dawn,' grinned Henry.

'I prefer brooms myself. Now if you'll excuse me, I'll just go and check on Robin before I sit down.'

Wes tiptoed into his son's room. It took him less than a second to see that the bed hadn't been slept in. He switched on the light. No boy.

He shot out of the bedroom and started checking all the other rooms in the cottage. 'He's not here!' he exclaimed. 'Robin's gone.'

'Don't panic,' said Henry, extricating himself with difficulty from the comfy depths of the armchair. 'Is there anywhere that he might have gone? A friend's place, perhaps? Like Luke's?'

'At this time of night? No. If he goes to Luke's house he's usually back by nine. It's almost ten.'

Henry opened his mouth to say, 'Let's ring Lou and check,' when Wes said, 'He's better not be with that Tonbridge woman!'

'Lou? How could he be?' said Henry, immediately changing tack because obviously mentioning Lou was not going to be a good idea. 'Lou was at the PTA meeting.'

'I wouldn't put it past her,' declared Wes. 'She's probably kidnapped him just to get at me.'

'Don't be ridiculous. She's got enough kids to contend with without kidnapping more!'

'She's crazy. I reckoned she'd resort to anything just to make my life more difficult.'

Headlights flashed into the driveway. 'That could be Robin now,' Henry said soothingly, wondering what on earth was going on between Wes and Lou. He'd seen them arguing that morning and again after the meeting.

That had actually been his main reason for gate-crashing his way into May Cottage. He'd wanted a private chat with Wes to find out exactly what was brewing between him and Lou Tonbridge.

Wes wrenched open the front door. Sally Bennett was standing there with her arm around a sleepy Robin.

'Mrs Bennett! You've found Robin!' Wes said swooping down on the boy. 'Where was he?'

'Don't fuss, Dad,' yawned Robin. 'I was just at Luke's house and fell asleep on the couch. It's no big deal.'

'I was baby-sitting at the Sommers's house,' said Sally with a calm smile. 'And I offered to bring him home.'

'So you weren't with Lou?' demanded Wes, still caught up with the idea that she was involved in enticing away his son.

'Lou isn't Mrs Sommers, Wes,' said Sally firmly, not giving Robin a chance to answer. She caught Henry's eye and gave him a challenging, arch look. 'Isn't that right, Henry.'

'Well, yes,' said Henry, rather puzzled but following Sally's lead anyway. 'That's right. Lou definitely is not Mrs Sommers.'

★ ★ ★

Lou yawned. She'd been up until one in the morning, typing Wes Drummond's reports, and she was bushed. It hadn't helped that although dog-tired, she had then lain in bed, eyes wide open and staring into the dark, thinking about her prickly employer.

He'd got under her skin, that much was for sure. And she didn't like it. It rankled that he disturbed her at a level she least expected or wanted.

Bother it, but she found him attractive.

OK, by Westerfield's standards — or anyone's standards come to that — Wes was definitely something special on the macho alpha male scale. Even Sally had called him a dish and she'd been married since forever.

But Lou knew she was attracted to Wes in spite of that. And in spite of his behaviour, in spite of the cruel, unfounded things he'd said about her and in spite of his insensitivity where his own son was concerned.

A man hadn't got her that rattled for years. OK, she had to admit that there hadn't been a man in her life for a long, long time. But that wasn't her fault. Circumstances beyond her control had conspired against her.

Three years ago, when she'd first taken on the boys, she'd soon discovered that nice, available men in the village were few and far between. And those that were kicking around soon backed off from her when they realised she came with strings attached, the strings being her nephews. As for her men friends in the city, she hadn't seen them for dust.

She gave a rueful smile. Being the guardian of five small boys was a big turn-off for any man, attractive or otherwise. No-one in their right mind wanted to be involved with a large, ready-made family.

In the beginning, she hadn't minded that much because she hadn't wanted involvement. She hadn't had the time or inclination. The boys were her focus.

But what about now?

Yes, she had to admit that now she was sometimes lonely. Not during the everyday razzmatazz of life, because there was barely time to think during the daylight hours. But she was lonely during the long nights. Lonely for a special someone to put his arms around her and share her thoughts and dreams and passions.

Passions. Hah. When had she last felt any degree of passion, except anger?

Which led her back to Wes Drummond. He made her flipping mad just about every time their paths crossed. Was she drawn to him because he'd ignited in her feelings stronger than her habitual acceptance of her lot?

Lou didn't know and she didn't think she ought to find out, because she was sure it would only end in tears. Neither of them was free to explore a relationship.

Wes Drummond was still getting to grips with his divorce and needed her like he needed root canal work without anaesthetic.

Lou groaned and covered her head with her pillow, trying to shut out images of Wes and smother the sudden urgent need surging within her.

It took her a long time to fall asleep and when she did she dreamed of a wild, cyclonic tempest. And Wes.

He was standing in the eye of the storm, the driving wind and rain surrounding him but not touching him. And he was holding his hand out towards her, urging her onwards. But, surprise, surprise, he was always just out of her reach.

★ ★ ★

The following day, after dropping the boys at their respective schools and Tom off at nursery, Lou drove to Sally's to deliver the reports and disks she'd had to prepare for Wes.

Once there, Sally wasted no time in telling Lou about the previous night's action and how she and Henry had covered for Lou.

'Henry knows?' Lou said, appalled. She plonked down into one of Sally's office chairs and dropped her head in her hands.

'Well, he doesn't know, per se, but he followed my lead like the perfect gentleman that Henry is.'

'This is getting more difficult by the day,' said Lou. 'But at least an end is in sight.' And she'd told Sally how Wes had insisted that he would pay for the Porsche repairs.

'So that's good, isn't it?' said Sally. 'If he's paying, you don't have to work for him anymore.'

Lou sort of felt it was good, but a part of her still wanted that contact with Wes, even though the night before she'd vowed to have nothing more to do with him.

'True,' she said with a sigh. 'I'll just do another week while you find someone else.'

'It might not be that easy to replace you,' said Sally, a frown puckering between her brows. 'With Christmas around the corner, lots of people are getting their homes and gardens spruced up and ready for the holidays. I don't have anyone free as yet.'

'Just see what you can do. I won't leave either you or the Drummonds in a fix. I'll work till you find a replacement. I'd best be off now or I won't get finished before nursery ends.'

'Just before you go,' said Sally with a wink. 'You might like to put your jumper on properly.'

Lou glanced down. Her red wool jumper was inside-out and back-to-front, showing all the seams and the size tag.

'Oh great,' she said tiredly. 'Good

luck. I'll change it once I'm at the cottage.'

* * *

Lou felt depressed as well as tired. She didn't want to go and clean at May Cottage. She didn't want to do anything that involved Wes Drummond. She'd much rather be at home, curled up with a cup of coffee and a good book, with Ollie at her feet and a crackling fire in the grate. But she was committed.

She left Sally's and drove slowly through the village, noting that the Porsche had gone from Joe's workshop.

Wes must have collected it that morning before going off to London for a day of meetings or business or whatever he did.

She didn't have a clue how he filled his days and she didn't want to know. The less she knew about Wes the better for her peace of mind.

Lou turned into the narrow lane

leading to May Cottage and cruised into the shady tree and shrub lined half-moon driveway, just as she did three mornings of the week.

Except this time it was different. This time the driveway was occupied.

Too late she saw the silver car parked under the yew tree. Too late she slammed on the bus's brakes and wrenched the steering wheel to one side.

Too soon, she hit the Porsche.

Lou groaned. That had blown it. Wes must have changed his plans and was home rather than in the city.

Which meant he would soon discover whom it was who worked for him — Lou-the-Porsche-Slayer.

'What the devil!' Wes flung out of the house like an angry Jack-in-a-box. He recoiled as soon as he saw the bus hanging off his car's back bumper.

'Dammit, Lou! What is it with you? If you're that keen to spend money on my car, then go ahead! Smash it all up, why don't you! Maybe you'd like to take it for a spin in a demolition derby. You'd win hands down, believe me.'

Lou got shakily out of the car. She felt sick to the pit of her stomach. Why was she such a klutz around him? Why couldn't she act sensibly? Why did things always have to go wrong?

'I'm sorry,' she said, her voice quivering like a struck tuning fork. 'I didn't expect you to be at home.'

'And that's an excuse?' He rammed his hands on his hips and stared down at her, icy eyes boring into her, waiting for an answer.

'No. Not really. I wasn't concentrating,' she said bleakly. 'And I was too tired to respond quickly.'

And then she surprised them both by bursting into tears.

Wes stared open-mouthed, which made Lou howl louder. Then his anger seemed to vaporise as quickly as summer rain on hot tarmac.

'Are you hurt?' he said awkwardly and reached out to touch her. Lou smacked his hand away.

She didn't want his sympathy. Instead, she wanted the ground to open up and swallow her whole.

She began hunting for a hanky in the capacious pockets of her baggy black tracksuit bottoms that she'd worn for comfort rather than style.

'Well I hope you're not crying to get my sympathy vote,' he said dryly. 'I expect better from you.'

'I'm not crying!' She wiped the backs of her hands over her wet face and searched up her red-woolly sleeves for any semblance of a tissue. 'I'm just . . . reacting,' she said lamely.

'It looks like common-or-garden old crying to me.' There was a tremor of laughter in his voice. 'Here, take my handkerchief. It's clean.'

He held out a white cotton handkerchief, again one of the items Lou had ironed earlier in the week.

Lou snatched it from his fingers and gave her nose a big squelchy blow and then mopped her brimming eyes. Thank goodness she hadn't been wearing mascara or she'd be looking like an insomniac panda who'd been on a weekend bender.

'Feeling better?'

'No. Yes. No. I'm sorry.'

'So am I, for shouting at you.'

'I deserved it. Just look what I've done to your lovely car now.'

Her eyes immediately sprung more leaks and fat tears made new tramlines down her cheeks.

'You're not going to start crying again, are you?' He sounded worried. As if a crying woman was a worse fate than a wrecked car.

'No! But look at it!'

They both turned and stared at the silver Porsche. The back end was all crumpled and resembled scrunched up tin-foil. The old red minibus was rammed against it tight, as if in a heated, passionate smooch, and didn't appear to have suffered that much damage except for a smashed headlight and slightly bent radiator.

'Joe had only just finished fixing the

Porsche,' she said and gave a very loud, watery sniff.

'It's just a car, Lou. No big deal.'

'That's not what you said the other day.'

'I think I'm getting used to it being bashed.'

'But your insurance premiums will go sky high. You'd best let me pay for the repairs this time.' She rubbed her forehead with her palm. Her head was sore and a knotty bump was swelling fast. She must have hit the windscreen when she'd braked. She felt bruised and sorry for herself. She soggily sniffed again.

'Look, you're all shaken up. Come in and have something to steady your nerves,' said Wes. His voice was kind and full of concern. It made Lou feel like bursting into fresh tears. She wasn't used to him being nice to her. She could handle his rage with equanimity but not his solicitude.

He tentatively put his hand on her arm, expecting her to brush him off again, but she meekly allowed him to guide her into the kitchen. He pushed her gently into the ash carver-chair that she'd polished with beeswax and vigour two days previously.

'What would you like?' he asked. 'Brandy? Whisky?'

'Good grief no! I'll never get through the day if I have a drink and I've got so much to do.'

'Relax. Don't think about later. Concentrate on now, on feeling better. How about tea? Coffee? Water?'

'A cup of coffee would be great. I need a caffeine fix.'

She was all jittery inside. Breakfast had been too long ago. Coffee would help steady her and stop her stomach suffering the waves of nervous tension.

Wes opened the cupboard and started searching for the coffee jar.

'Top left cupboard, second shelf,' Lou supplied after watching him rummage through her carefully laid out cupboards. She blew her nose again as he followed her instructions. He took out the jar and then began searching for a clean mug.

'Bottom cupboard middle shelf,' said Lou automatically, just like she did with the boys when they were scrabbling through the farmhouse kitchen cupboards searching for things.

She took a deep, steadying breath and tried to get her act together. This was daft, feeling so churned-up. It was just a stupid accident after all. No life had been lost. No bones had been broken. Wes was right. It was just a car. Even if it was a Porsche.

She absently watched him open the crockery cupboard where she'd stowed the Drummonds' minimal amount of chinaware when she'd unpacked their boxes a month ago.

Wes suddenly stopped what he was doing. He turned and gave her a very hard stare.

What? Why was he looking at her like that? Was it because of her stupid jumper being inside-out? She should really have changed it at Sally's. Or perhaps her bump had grown to the size of a goose egg?

'How did you know where everything is?' he said in a quiet, measured tone.

'What do you mean?'

'You knew where the coffee and mugs were kept.'

Lou experienced a swish-back style sickening feeling in her belly that was as bad as her reaction to hitting the Porsche.

Uh-oh. She hadn't been concentrating again. In her turmoil over the accident she'd been caught out. And if Wes hadn't been angry a moment ago, he certainly was now.

She briefly thought about lying and saying she'd just made lucky guesses but judging by his darkening, suspicious expression she doubted if he'd believe her. No, she'd have to be upfront.

'Because I put them there. I'm your cleaner, Wes. That's why I came here this morning. It's one of my regular cleaning days.'

Her voice shook slightly and she took a deep breath to calm herself down, while her fingers curled tight around the smooth polished arms of the chair for courage.

She decided that she might as well go quietly and with dignity. 'And I quite understand if you want to fire me on the spot,' she said.

Silence hung in the kitchen like cold skin on thick custard. Lou steeled herself for his outburst, clenching her hands harder around the worn ashwood arms of the chair, dipping her head to avoid the arctic fury she was sure she'd witnessed in his eyes.

'Come again?' he said after what felt like a lifetime.

Lou lifted her head and stared unwaveringly at him. He didn't look angry, just confused. Very.

'I'm your cleaner.'

'But that's Louisa. Louisa? Lou? Oh no! I don't believe it! I should have known!'

'And I'm your gardener.' She paused

a beat. 'And your secretary.' It was best, she decided, to get everything out in the open.

'Good grief.' The kettle began to shrilly whistle. Wes impatiently snapped it off and then glared at her. 'Why the devil didn't you tell me before?' His voice was clipped and flinty.

'The subject never arose.'

'But you've been stomping all over my house . . . '

'And garden.'

'And garden. And typing my business reports. And you've never once said.' His fury began to unfurl, his face tightening, his eyes becoming electrically charged.

Lou swallowed painfully. What was he going to do? Physically pick her up and hurl her out of the door?

'You've been in my bedroom and study and gone through my personal things!'

'I know what sock size you take, what you eat for breakfast, what toothpaste you use and which words you spell

107

incorrectly. It's too late, Wes. I know you intimately.'

Now why had she said that? The knock on her head must have rattled her senses. Now he looked fit to explode. It was time to get out of here.

She rose to leave but her legs felt all rubbery, whether because of the accident or his anger, she wasn't quite certain, but she had to sit back down again before she fell over.

'Blast! Are you one of those sad women who like to stalk men?' Disbelief now warred with his anger.

He was seriously disturbed, she realised, and she gave a derisive snort. 'I don't have time to stalk! I barely have time to pluck my eyebrows. I took all three jobs because I needed the money. It's as simple as that.'

She didn't add that she'd needed the money to pay for his Porsche repairs. That would have been flapping a red rag in front of a very grumpy bull and he was mad enough.

'You've been secretly skulking around

my home for weeks!'

'You've been paying me to clean your house, maintain your garden and type your reports. There was nothing secretive about it. And for the record, I have never skulked in my life!'

'You've invaded my privacy.'

'Legitimately. You hired me. I've been washing and ironing your shirts, cooking your meals, stripping your bed.'

'I think you'd better leave,' said Wes with a biting civility that shattered her vision and landed her back to earth with a crash.

She rallied quickly, cross with herself for getting sidetracked. 'What? Without my coffee? You're not a very sensitive employer. What about duty of care?'

'This isn't the time for flippancy, Louisa! You're fired. I want you out of my house and out of my life. Now!'

'Fine.' Lou stood and ignored the quivering of her limbs. She made it outside without collapsing on the floor, so that was something. She got into the bus, took a very, very deep breath and then reversed off the Porsche's bumper with lots of loud and expensive screeches.

She then drove away without looking back.

6

It was Saturday. Wes was in the middle of a big, bustling supermarket and was trying, not very successfully, to do his weekly shop. He'd forgotten his shopping list and he just couldn't remember what they'd run out of and which stocks were running low.

They probably needed bread, cheese and eggs, as that seemed to be their staple diet at the moment, but for the life of him he didn't know what else.

He'd sent Robin off to find the shampoo and soap and anything else he thought they might need. That had been a while ago. He hoped Robin hadn't got lost or been arrested by the security guard for suspicious behaviour. It was more likely the boy was hiding from him. He didn't blame him. Wes had been grouchy and morose since his confrontation with Lou.

He still felt mad at her for her under-handedness. Why hadn't she told him she worked for him, for heavens sake? What was the big deal about keeping it secret?

Because, came the uncomfortable reply from his conscience, you're prejudiced and would have sacked her on the spot.

Wes ground his teeth. So? She still should have been upfront. But instead, she'd tricked him. He was completely within his rights to be angry with her.

In the weeks she'd been working for him, she'd made herself indispensable — either purposefully or accidentally, he didn't care which — and he'd come to rely on her.

Now he missed her lip-smacking casseroles, the crisp clean sheets, the sweet smelling towels and the womanly touches that made the cottage feel like a real home and not some bachelor doss-house.

And, Wes had to be honest, he missed their spats even more. Lou had made him feel more alive and human than he had done since his marriage had ended.

What was it about the crazy woman with her wild hair and large sensitive eyes that had pierced his armour and snagged his interest?

Wes sighed. Well, whatever it was he'd blown it. Now he was back to an untidy cottage and unappetising meals. It hadn't taken long for the cottage to fall into disarray.

How could two people make so much mess? He'd never thought of himself as a disorganised person, but he was certainly making a hash of running May Cottage.

He couldn't even remember what he had to buy. He racked his brains, trying to visualise the fridge and pantry and mentally work out what was needed.

But he knew what he needed.

And that made him even grumpier. Because he needed Lou!

But like the contrary woman she was, she'd taken him at his word and had absented herself from his life. Big time. He hadn't seen her at the school grounds or around the village.

He'd taken to popping into the village store on the flimsiest of excuses just to see if she might be there. But she hadn't been. He hadn't even seen her bus parked about the place. The woman had all but disappeared.

Now he picked up a packet of cornflakes and threw it into the trolley. He followed it with oats and bran because he vaguely thought they'd be good for fibre. He then began searching for the pasta.

As he rounded the aisle where all the Christmas chocolates and candy canes were displayed he suddenly saw her.

Emotion surged like a wild beast in his breast. One side of him wanted to race over to her and beg her to come back into his life. The other half warred against such action, still mad at her for exercising her subterfuge for whatever dubious motives she'd had.

He jerked back his trolley and hid

behind a big cardboard cut-out advertising Christmas stocking chocolate packs.

He peeked around the chocolate stand and saw Lou surrounded by boys of various sizes.

And then the boys broke ranks and he realised that his own son was standing in the midst of the rowdy group. Lou had an arm around him and was regarding him with that Wes could only describe as affection.

She was cuddling his son! Again! And after he'd expressly forbidden it!

Wes didn't like the scene one bit.

Anger swamped any other emotion that Wes was feeling and he saw red.

Hardly realising what he was doing, he shoved the cardboard advertisement away and bellowed at the top of his voice, 'Louisa Tonbridge, let go of my son!'

Behind him the cut-out fell to the floor with a clatter and startled shoppers turned to stare. Wes didn't care. He wanted that woman away from his boy.

'You're a menace, Lou. I told you not to go anywhere near Robin,' he shouted, marching straight up to her.

Lou's mouth dropped open in shock, but she kept her arm firmly around Rob. The other boys crowded around her like a protective shield. They were more intimidating than a pride of stockbrokers. Give Wes a boardroom full of high flyers any day.

He checked his stride and jabbed a finger in Lou's direction. 'Let him go.'

'I'm not hurting him, Mr Drummond.'

'I said, let go!'

'Fine.' Lou patted Rob's shoulder and then gently pushed him forwards towards Wes. 'You'd better go with your dad before he has a coronary,' she said.

'But Auntie Lou . . . . .'

Auntie Lou? 'She's not your aunt!' bellowed Wes.

'She's like an aunt to me, Dad.'

Lou frowned at Wes to be quiet and pushed Rob again. 'Go on, Rob. It's OK.'

He still hung back.

Wes noted his reluctance and his anger cranked up even further. 'I thought I told you to stay away from my son!'

'I can't exactly avoid him in a public place,' said Lou.

'You don't have to put your arms around him!'

'You're causing a scene,' said Lou, embarrassed.

'I don't care.'

'But I do. You're upsetting the boys.'

'I'm not upset, Auntie Lou,' piped up Caleb. 'This man always shouts at us.'

Wes stared at the boy in astonishment. The boy calmly stared back.

'Yes, he does,' chipped in Toby. 'And he makes us late for school.'

'I . . . ' Wes was temporarily bereft of words.

'Yes, well we won't discuss it now,' said Lou hastily, eyeing Wes with trepidation but pleased to see that the boys' comments had effectively silenced him. 'I've still got to get the bread rolls for the bonfire party tonight, so if you'll excuse me, Mr Drummond.'

'Dad, can I help Auntie Lou with the hotdog stand?'

'No! And she's not your Auntie Lou!'

'But it's for the school. We'll be there anyway and I'd really like to help.'

'I don't want you anywhere near this woman, Robbie.'

'But Dad.'

'It's OK, Rob. There'll be plenty of people helping me. You just enjoy the night with your dad. Now I must get on. I've got lots to do before tonight.'

Lou pushed past him with the trolley and headed for the bakery department.

She didn't look back. She didn't dare. It was bad enough that her legs were wobbling and her pulse rate was up. That man had a bad effect on her!

★ ★ ★

That night the villagers turned out in force. Many of them were in fancy dress to lend colour and spectacle to the

118

bonfire society's procession. Some were carrying torches to light the massive bonfire on the village green. Others were rugged up in warm coats, hats and scarves.

Lou, a bright green woolly hat pulled over her frizzy curls, was already cooking up a storm at the hotdog stand. Charcoal burners flared and the mouth-watering smell of sausages and onions filled the cold night air.

Henry was next to her and was dressed for action in a blue striped apron. They were doing a brisk trade.

'So where are all the other willing helpers?' remarked Henry. Flipping the onions and making them spit.

'Keeping well away from us,' laughed Lou. 'What do you expect? It's the same every year.'

'Well, I'm going to press-gang some of the parents into helping. It's not fair that it always comes down to you.'

'You were the one who dobbed me in, Henry!'

'You could have said no.'

'And be lynched by the PTA? I don't think so.'

'It's still not right. I'll be back in a jiffy with some reinforcements.'

He was back quicker than Lou expected and her heart sank when she saw whom he had in tow.

'Wes volunteered to give you a hand,' said Henry, beaming. He took off his apron and handed it to Wes. 'Now you two carry on while I drum up some other willing and not-so-willing workers.'

'Oh boy,' said Lou as Henry disappeared into the crowd. 'He doesn't realise what he's done.'

'Henry's no fool,' said Wes, tying the apron around his waist. 'He knows exactly what he's doing.'

'Meaning?'

'He has an idea that you and I should hit it off.'

'I think I've had enough collisions with you to last a lifetime,' said Lou tartly. 'You don't have to stay, you know. I'm perfectly able to run this stall on my own.'

'And face Henry's ire? No thank you. I'd rather get a spatula in the ribs from you.'

'Hmph. Henry's a sweetie. He wouldn't get cross with anyone.'

'Don't you believe it. He ticked me off for shouting at you in the supermarket.'

'He did?' Lou could feel her face burn with embarrassment. Thank goodness it was dark. But how many other friends and villagers had witnessed their confrontation? She shuddered. It didn't bear thinking about.

'And Sally gave me a good old-fashioned tongue-lashing too. And so did Joe the mechanic. So really you could say that I'm in the villagers' bad books.'

'Serves you right,' Lou muttered under her breath. Bring back the stocks and dunking in the village pond! But she was touched by her friends' burst of solidarity. It gave her a nice warm, fuzzy feeling.

'And even without their admonishments, I was feeling terrible. I acted like

121

a right twit. I owe you an apology, Lou. I was totally out of order. I just hope you can forgive me.'

'Oh. Well . . . '

He'd unbalanced her. Lou wasn't expecting Wes to be nice to her.

'I was just so cross to see you on such easy terms with Robin. Especially after telling you to keep away from him. But I didn't mean to be so heavy about it.'

Lou nervously hopped from one boot-clad foot to the other as Wes carried on talking in a low, intense voice as he poked at the sizzling onions with Henry's pair of tongs.

'I was overreacting,' he said. 'Robin doesn't show me any affection, you see, and I suppose I was jealous.'

Jealous? OK, she could understand that. She'd probably be jealous if her nephews started hugging other people.

'And if I'm honest, I wasn't just jealous that he was being affectionate to somebody else.'

'No?'

'No, I was jealous because I wanted it to be me who was being hugged . . . ' He paused. ' . . . by you.'

Lou gasped and dropped the sausage she was turning. It fell on to the charcoal and whooshed up in flames. Just like her cheeks.

Wes stabbed the onions some more. 'And I've missed you,' he said, almost inaudibly so that Lou wasn't quite sure that she'd heard right above the popping and splattering of the incinerating sausage.

'Sorry?'

Wes raised his head and stared straight at her.

'I've missed you. Missed our . . . er . . . interesting discussions.'

Missed her! Whoa! How had this happened? What was going on? Lou thought he was just apologising for the supermarket incident. But obviously not!

She didn't know quite how to respond and was glad that she didn't have to say anything immediately because a crowd of teenagers fronted up at the stall.

Lou and Wes spent the next few minutes serving them and then Lou threw on some more sausages and cast a wary eye at Wes. He caught her glance and quirked a smile.

'So am I forgiven?' he said.

'Well, yes. I suppose so.' What else could she say, but it came out as more of a croak.

'And we'll declare a cease-fire?'

'For what it's worth.' She found it difficult to speak because her heart was yammering so hard it was almost jumping up into her throat and gagging her. She felt as though her whole world had tilted on its axis and she was about to fall off into space.

Perhaps now was the time she should come clean about Rob visiting the farm? Surely he'd forgive her for not telling him, now that they seemed to be on better terms and all?

Wes's smile became a little rueful and then he said, 'And please can I have a hug too?'

Now she was definitely falling and

spiralling into space!

The next moment she was in his arms and it wasn't Lou doing the hugging at all. It was Wes. And he held her oh-so-close. And it had been such a long, long time since she'd been held by a man that she almost passed out by the unexpected strength of emotion that coursed through her.

Then Wes pulled off her woolly hat and buried his fingers into her hair. 'I've been wanting to do that ever since I first saw you,' he said with a whisper.

'You have? I thought you wanted to strangle me!' She decided to opt for the jokey, casual note to mask the intensity of her feelings. It might help her try and ignore the way her blood was a churning torrent. But it didn't. It was all consuming.

'I wanted to do that too.' He gave a low chuckle and that made her blood flow even faster. 'And this.' And he dipped his head and softly kissed her on the lips.

Oh my, thought Lou. I'm done for.

Then she gave into the moment and closed her eyes and kissed him back for her didn't know how long.

A tentative cough brought them crashing back to earth.

'Sorry to interrupt,' said Henry. 'But the sausages are burning.'

'Oh no!' Lou jumped back from Wes and hurriedly began removing the charred food from the grill. Wes chuckled and Henry discreetly faded back into the crowd.

'That was your fault,' she tossed over her shoulder at Wes.

'For once I agree with you.'

'So stop laughing and help me!'

They worked together in silence, salvaging as many of the sausages as possible. Lou was in too much turmoil to say anything and Wes seemed content with her silence.

But though Lou was quiet, her brain was in a din of confusion. He'd kissed her! Kissed her! She hadn't expected such a development in their relationship. OK, the sparks always flew but was that why? Because they were attracted to each other?

But it couldn't go any further until she'd confessed about Robin's visits. How could she broach the subject? She hadn't a clue, but it had to be done before things became even more complicated.

Lou gathered her courage and opened her mouth to speak only to shut it again as her nephews and Robin bounded up to the stall.

'We're starving, Auntie Lou,' said Luke. 'Please can we have some hotdogs?'

'Of course you can, Luke,' said Lou, glad of the diversion. 'Hotdogs all round, what do you say, Wes?' She tossed a look at him and her heart lurched to a halt. Wes was staring at her as if she'd suddenly grown two heads. 'What?' she said. 'What's wrong?' But she knew what was wrong. She'd been pipped at the post. She would have told him weeks ago . . .

'Luke,' he said.

'Yes?'

'Luke is your nephew?'

'Yes.'

Feverishly she began shovelling sausages and onions into rolls, squirting them with tomato sauce and handing them to the boys.

'Not Luke Sommers, by an coincidence?'

'Well, yes.' She had two more hotdogs to go before the storm burst.

'I don't suppose his mother is around here somewhere?' A steely menace had crept into his voice and Lou shivered. The cease-fire was over.

'No. She's not. The boys are orphans.' She handed the last hotdog to Rob and flashed the boy a quick, comforting smile. 'Off you all go, boys, or you'll miss the fireworks,' she said with false brightness.

Wes watched them go and then said, 'And you are?'

'I think you know who I am, Wes. I'm their aunt. And their guardian.'

'You called yourself Mrs Sommers!'

128

'No, you called me that and I just didn't bother correcting you.'

'So you lied.'

'No! Well, not exactly.'

'My son has been coming around to your house just about every night of the week the entire term.'

'Yes.' There was no arguing the point.

'And yet you knew I didn't want him seeing you.'

'Well, yes.'

'So you defied me as well as lied to me.'

'Well, yes but . . . '

'Were you ever going to tell me?'

'I was waiting for the right moment,' she said lamely.

'Or you've been trying to worm your way into my life for some devious reason of your own.'

'That's ridiculous!' she said, surprised and stung.

'Soft-soaping my boy, making yourself indispensable in my home,' he carried on. 'What did you hope to achieve, Ms Tonbridge? Reckoned you'd snare me?

Did you see me as a convenient meal ticket for you and the boys? Did the Porsche turn your head and you thought there was more where that came from? Well sorry, sweetheart, you're out of luck. Marina has already cleaned me out. You've been sold a dud.'

'You're being insulting!'

'But I'm right!'

'If that's what you want to believe, buster, then that's fine with me,' she seethed.

Wes stared at her, a sudden bleakness in his eyes. 'I'm disappointed in you, Lou. I thought you had integrity. I was wrong. You played me for a fool.'

'You're not the only fool here,' Lou muttered under her breath, feeling her heart cracking under her ribs and her lifeblood seeping away.

Wes threw down the tongs. 'I forbid you or your nephews to have anything more to do with Robin.'

With that he left, passing Henry as he strode away into the night.

'Goodness,' said Henry. 'What's up

with Wes now? And you for that matter,' he added seeing her taut, thin-lipped face. 'I thought you two were getting on so well. In fact I thought you were enjoying your own private fireworks!'

'Very funny, Henry.'

'So? What's gone wrong this time?'

'Wes found out that the person he thought was Mrs Sommers was me.'

'Oh, dear.'

'And I've just burnt the rest of the sausages.'

7

Lou was jolted out of a deep, deep sleep by the ringing of the telephone and she cursed herself for forgetting to switch on the answering machine before going to bed. She tottered in the dark down the stairs, stubbed her toe on the kitchen doorjamb, hit the light switch and then switched up the receiver, hoping the strident ringing hadn't woken the boys.

'Yes?' she whispered, squinting against the bright light and wincing as she rubbed her sore toe.

'Have you kidnapped my son?' Wes Drummond's accusation flew down the line and made Lou wince even more. She held the receiver away from her ear as he carried on about her underhanded dealings where his family was concerned.

When she was sure he'd stopped

shouting, she said, 'Get real, Wes, of course, I haven't kidnapped Rob.' She yawned and rubbed her eyes with the knuckles of one hand. Her feet were freezing on the flag-stoned kitchen floor and she wished she'd taken time to throw on her dressing-gown and slippers. She had a feeling this was going to take some time.

'Then where is he?' Lou heard the crack of panic and her heart softened in spite of being cross with him for waking her up and yelling at her. He was worried about Rob. Who could blame him for shouting?

'I don't know, but I'll go and check the house if you like.'

'Please. And Lou, please be quick. I need to find him.'

'Of course you do. I'll be quick as I can.' Lou padded about the house and made a thorough search. Robin wasn't there. On the way back to the phone she glanced at the kitchen clock.

'Do you know it's gone midnight, Wes?'

'So?'

'So are you really sure he's not fast asleep in his bed and snoring under the bedclothes?'

'Would I be ringing you if that was the case?' he snapped.

'No. Sorry. I wasn't thinking.' Hardly surprising as she was still half asleep! 'Anyway, he's not here.'

'You've searched everywhere?'

'Yes.'

'Are you sure?'

'Yes!'

He swore and again Lou forgave him, because he sounded near breaking point.

'I've been driving around the village for hours. There's no sign of him.'

'When did he go missing?'

'After the bonfire.'

'He's probably gone off with some friends, then, and forgotten the time or something.' She knew it sounded weak but what else could she suggest?

'No. He hasn't.'

'No?'

'We argued.'

'Oh.' Well that changed things. 'And?'

'He overheard me arguing with you at the hotdog stand and then told me that if he had to choose between the two of us, he'd choose you.'

Lou closed her eyes. Uh-oh.

'I'm sure he didn't mean it, Wes. He was just lashing out. He was angry with you and wanted to punish you.'

'The thing is, Lou, I think he's made the right choice.' The fight suddenly went out of his voice and he sounded defeated. 'I'm one lousy father.'

Lou took a deep breath. It was one thing dealing with an insecure teenager, but his dad too? 'Now's not the time to feel sorry for yourself, Wes,' she said briskly. 'Think about this logically. He's got to be somewhere close by.' She nibbled her lower lip as she thought of places where Robin might have gone.

'I'm out of ideas.'

'OK. Let me think.' She threw out a few possibilities, but Wes fielded them as already looked into or impossible.

'I don't suppose he would try and make it to his mother's place in France?'

'Maybe.' Wes sounded doubtful. 'But he didn't have much money on him.'

'He could hitch.'

Wes swore again and ranted on about the dangers of hitching rides.

'But he probably hasn't,' she tried to stem the flow before he completely went off the deep-end. 'I'll go and wake up Luke. He might have some idea of where he is. I'll ring you back in a minute.'

Luke was dead to the world and it took Lou a few moments of shaking and hissing in his ear to wake him up.

'Do you know where Rob is?' she whispered and flashed the torch in his face to gauge his reaction.

The boy buried his face under the covers. 'Leave it out, Auntie Lou. You're blinding me.'

Lou dragged the bedclothes off again and trained the torch back on his face. 'I need to know, Luke. It's urgent. Do you know where he is?'

''Course not.' His eyes slid away from hers and Lou knew he was lying.

'Luke, the police will have to be called if we don't find him,' she said gently. 'It's best you tell me if you know.'

'Aaw, Auntie Lou. Just leave him be. He's OK.'

'Where is he?'

'He didn't want to go home. I thought he'd be safer here.'

'Where here?'

'In the barn.'

'Thank you. I think.'

'Will I get into trouble?'

'With Mr Drummond? Maybe.' She would but that was something entirely different. Wes would hold her responsible and no doubt drag in the authorities just like he'd threatened before. She shivered. It didn't bear thinking about.

'Nah, Auntie Lou. Mr Drummond might shout a lot but he doesn't scare me. No, I meant with you.'

'Well, sweetie, it's not the best thing you've done lately. You should have taken me into your confidence. But we'll talk about it in the morning. Now go to sleep.'

'I'd rather come and get Rob with you. He won't want to face his dad on his own.'

'But I'll be there.'

'Yeah, but I want to be too. Safety in numbers and all that.'

He had a point. Lou knew first hand how furious Wes could get.

While Luke put on his dressing gown, Lou rang Wes and told him that Robin was safe. She then went to the barn with Luke. Rob was asleep in Luke's sleeping bag on a pile of old hessian sacks. There was a pile of half-eaten food from her fridge by his side. At least she now knew where the cold sausages for the boys' school lunches had gone.

By the time Lou had woken Rob and made him and Luke a hot chocolate, Wes was banging on her back door.

'Sshh! You'll wake everybody up,' she admonished, cracking open the door and pushing Wes backwards into the chilly night.

She then quietly closed the door behind her.

'Where he is? Is he OK?' He tried to sidestep her but Lou was too fast. She held out her hand to ward him off.

'He's fine, but I don't want you marching in there and going off like a Chinese fire cracker. Let's be civilised about this.'

'But, Lou, I want to see him!'

'Yes, but I don't want you yelling at him. It won't do either of you any good. And you might wake up the little ones,' she added for good measure. She dropped her hand and hunched herself further into the old plaid dressing gown. It wasn't much protection against the icy night air and she shivered.

'Hey, come here.' Wes suddenly enveloped her in his arms. 'You're freezing.'

'I'm OK.' But he didn't listen to her protest and folded her into his warmth. It was unnerving and wonderful all at the same time.

Wes rested his head on the top of hers. 'I was about to blow it again with Rob, wasn't I?' He sounded contrite.

'Yep.'

'Tell it how it is, Lou.'

'Always.'

'So what should I do?'

'Go in there and say sorry.'

He bridled at that and held her slightly away from him. 'But I'm not the one who ran off.'

'But you were the one who caused the head-on.'

'I'm his dad. I make the rules.'

'But you're alienating him. Ease up.'

'So what do you suggest? A complete about face?'

'No. I appreciate that a man like you wouldn't be happy doing that.'

'A man like me? What's that supposed to mean?' Now he dropped his arms completely. He rammed his hands on his hips and scowled at her.

Oops. Lou hadn't intended to say that. 'Well, you know what I mean,' she said quickly. 'Aim for a compromise. I know you don't care for me very much . . . '

And then she remembered that she'd just been in his arms. And that earlier they'd had a heated encounter at the hotdog stand.

She blushed rosily and was thankful that the darkness hid her reddened cheeks.

' . . . but I'm not as bad as you think I am,' she continued too breathlessly for comfort.

'I don't think you're bad,' he countered. 'Just . . . '

She didn't let him finish, not wanting to know exactly what he thought. Just in case she didn't like it.

'Well, whatever you think, why don't you let Rob come around occasionally and be with my boys. They get on well and he enjoys being here.'

'How often is occasionally?'

'Two or three times a week?'

'Two or three?'

'He's been coming five at least.'

'Grief. I had no idea.'

'Don't worry about it. We enjoy having him here. But if you want to warn him off from us, please do it gently. For all our sakes.'

Lou held her breath, waiting, hoping that he wouldn't sever all ties. She didn't want Rob to stop seeing the boys.

And she definitely didn't want to stop seeing Wes, however bad he was for her peace of mind.

Wes scuffed the floor with his booted foot while he considered what she'd said. 'I don't know about the weaning off,' he finally said.

'Two nights won't kill you,' she pleaded.

Wes glanced up and in the darkness Lou was sure he grinned. 'OK, let's make it at least two.'

'Deal.'

Wes held out his hand and they

shook on it. Then he said, 'And I'm coming too. Why should Rob have all the fun?'

'You too?' Lou gawped in a mixture of alarm and excitement. 'Fun?'

'And I don't think weaning Robin off your family is the way to go.'

'You don't? But you just made a deal!'

'I reckon adopting the two of us would be better! I think it's time I spent a lot more time with you and the boys.' He glinted at her in the dark. 'I'm game if you are, Lou.'

With that he pushed past her and strode into the house. Oh goodness, thought Lou. And suddenly she didn't know if she could cope!

★ ★ ★

Tuesday night loomed. Lou had showered, changed her top at least three times. She'd been trying, not very successfully, to strike the best balance between no-nonsense-everyday-wear and

143

feminine-attractive-vamp. She'd even fixed her hair in an attempt to look marginally less wild and woolly.

Wes had always seen her at her worst. Lou was determined to present a more mature, woman-of-the-world image. She had been one once. She couldn't have lost her touch completely. But gazing at herself in the full-length mirror in her bedroom, Lou wondered if she had.

She looked exactly what she was; a tired skinny wreck with frizzy hair that needed a good cut and clothes that needed to be put in the ragbag.

But it was too late to do anything about it. They would arrive at any moment. She smoothed on some more mousse and touched up the lipstick. There was no two ways about it; Lou was jittery about having Wes under her roof. He'd made it clear that he was interested in her. But what did he want? An affair? It would be too much to expect that he wanted more.

'Something smells good,' said Wes when Luke ushered the Drummonds into the kitchen a few moments later.

'I've done a roast,' said Lou and blushed like a gauche schoolgirl as Wes handed her a bottle of wine and kissed her cheek.

'Auntie Lou's the best cook in the world,' said Rob and he kissed the other cheek so as not to be outdone.

Wes raised his brows and Lou spun around to stir the gravy.

'Since when do you go around kissing women?' Wes said to Robin.

'Auntie Lou's not 'women'. She's family,' said Rob and then hugged her into the bargain.

'Yes, well,' said Lou stammering and blushing even more and hoping that Wes wouldn't hug her too and reduce her to jelly. 'Let's set the table and eat.'

The meal was the usual noisy affair with all the boys vying to be heard and all demanding Lou's attention. Only Wes was quiet. When the boys started to clear the table ready to wash up, Wes excused them.

'Don't worry, boys, I'll help Auntie

Lou to clear up.'

'That's not the deal,' said Rob. 'We do it.'

'Not tonight. My treat.' The boys didn't need to be told twice and left the room. Silence descended like a blanket of snow and Lou felt suddenly shy at being alone with him. She shifted in her chair and twiddled with her empty wine glass.

'Relax,' said Wes. 'Have another glass of wine and take things easy while I wash up.'

'But . . . '

'Do you argue about everything, Lou?'

'Not usually.'

'Then why do you with me?'

'I don't!'

'There you go again.'

'OK. I'm sorry. You can do all the washing and drying up yourself. You can even do the vacuuming if you want!'

'That's more like it,' he chuckled. He stacked the plates and filled the sink with hot water. Then he said, 'I've got a long overdue apology to make.'

'You have?'

'Yes. I've been seriously wrong about you. I was too caught up in my own troubles to view things clearly and was overreacting when things didn't go my way. You've been a lifeline to Robin. And to me. I really appreciate everything you've done, Lou.'

She shrugged, embarrassed by his sudden earnestness.

'And you've made a great home here. You handle the kids well.'

'I've had a lot of practise.'

'It can't have been easy.'

A sudden lump formed in Lou's throat. She hadn't experienced a surge of grief for such a long time and it took her by surprise.

She stared into her wine glass, struggling to compose herself, unaware that Wes had stopped washing up and was closely watching her.

'It wasn't,' she finally said. 'But as you're finding as a single parent, there's no going back. You have to survive, for everyone's sake.'

'Yeah. I don't think I'm doing such a good job as you.' He returned to the dishes.

'Don't put yourself down, Wes. I had some terrible times early on. But I've been doing it for three years now. If I can cope, you can too. You'll probably find the crisis with Rob is over. There'll be other trials, but the worst is over.'

'Maybe.'

'Take it from one who's been there. You can do it but it does take time and commitment.'

'But he loves you and the family more than me.'

'He loves the stability. And that's what he needs from you. To be there. Most, if not all, of the time.'

'I'm trying.'

'Show him you are. Tell him. Work with him.'

Nothing was said for a few moments and then Wes said, 'Don't you ever get lonely, Lou?'

The softening of his tone made Lou tense and feel all hot and bothered. Her heart rate kicked up a pace and her pulse skittered. 'The boys are good company,' she said, annoyed she sounded a little husky. 'And I have a lot of close friends.'

Wes took his sudsy hands out of the sink and turned around to face her, dripping bubbles and water on the flagstones. 'Rob's good company too and I have a lot of friends, but I'm still lonely. It doesn't replace having someone special in your life.'

'I've never been married,' Lou hedged, wiggling nervously in her chair. 'So I've got nothing to compare it with.'

'But you've had relationships before you took on the boys.'

'Yes. But not serious ones. And the men all disappeared once I moved in here. Not that I blame them,' she added. 'It was to be expected.'

'Anyone since.'

'That's none of your business.'

He ignored her frown. 'The village

grapevine says not.'

'Sally Bennett should keep her mouth shut.'

'Why do you think it was Sally?'

'Because she's a matchmaker.'

'Actually it was Joe and Josh and Henry, as well as several other people.'

Lou sighed in defeat. 'No-one in their right mind would take on a woman with five boys.'

'Does that worry you?'

'Yes. Sometimes,' she admitted. 'I love the boys to pieces, but I'd love to have my own babies too.'

'How many?'

'One, maybe two. So you see, it would be a brave man to take me on.'

'Not if he loved you.'

Suddenly the air crackled with searing tension. The electricity that had been evident at all their meetings was charging up to high voltage. Lou gripped the stem of her wineglass so tightly that it was in danger of snapping.

'Well,' she said lamely. 'Well . . . '

And then the magic moment was broken by the ring of the front door bell. Lou could have wept.

But who in dickens was using the front door? No-one did. Ever. She heard the boys run to open the door and the next moment a glamorous blonde woman whooshed into the kitchen and launched herself at Wes.

'Darling,' she said and kissed Wes full on the mouth. 'I was told by the local garage owner that I'd find you here.'

'Marina! What are you doing here?' Wes automatically returned her embrace.

'I've come home!'

'Home?'

'It's where I should have been all along,' she gushed, leaning against his chest and gazing up at him with huge blue eyes. 'And when you rang me to say Robbie had run away, I realised how selfish I'd been. So I'm back and we can be one happy family again. And this time we'll make it work. Promise.'

Lou turned away.

She felt sick and hollow inside.

For a few wild moments she'd believed that there was a chance that Wes had cared for her. The idea had made her zing like she'd never done before. But that brief, precious hope had expired in an instant.

Because Marina had come home to reclaim her man.

'Lou, let me introduce you to Marina, my ex-wife,' said Wes, breaking in on her unhappiness.

'Ex-wife indeed,' laughed Marina. 'Don't be so pompous.'

'But you are. The divorce went through months ago,' he said mildly.

'Oh, that's just a silly piece of paper!' she announced and smiled at Lou. 'So pleased to meet you. I've heard so much about you from Robbie.' She linked an arm around her son who was standing, round-eyed, at her side.

Lou managed to summon a crooked smile. 'Rob's talked about you too, Marina. What a great Christmas present to have you back home. We were just having a glass of wine. Would you like one or are you in a hurry to leave?'

'Thank you, darling, but I think we should go home.'

Was it Lou's imagination or did Marina put a great deal of emphasis on the word 'home'?

'There's so much to discuss,' laughed Marina, patting Wes's cheeks and blowing him an air kiss.

Lou risked a glance at Wes. His face was an impersonal mask. He was back to being the cool, implacable stranger she'd first met and Lou felt she was dying inside.

Marina blew kisses to all the boys and left the house in a flurry, holding Wes' arm. He helped her settle into her hire car and then said, 'I've left my jacket,' and he returned to the kitchen, pulling Lou back into the house with him.

'Lou, I had no idea she'd come back,' he said, his voice low and urgent. 'It doesn't change anything.'

'There was nothing to change,' Lou replied bleakly.

'You know there was. Is.'

'Your wife is back, Wes. You've a second chance to make things work. For Rob's sake, if not yours. There's nothing else to say.'

'Lou.'

'Go. Please.'

She closed her eyes to stem the sudden spurt of tears and felt the briefest brush of his lips on hers and then the door shut. A few seconds later she heard the roar of the two cars and then the boys came pouring back into the kitchen.

'Well,' said Luke.

'Well,' said Lou and blew her nose. She wanted a good howl, but this wasn't time for self-indulgence. 'Who's going to finish the washing up for me?'

8

The next few weeks were purgatory for Lou. Marina, beautiful, graceful and capable, was everywhere. She got involved with the school's Christmas fayre. She joined the church choir. And she helped sell tickets for the village pantomime. Everybody loved her. She was the bubbly life and soul of Westerfield.

Even Lou admired her, though she'd ruined Lou's hopes and dreams. Marina had a kind word for everyone and was prepared to pitch in with village life.

The only cloud was Marina's insistence that Robin spend more time at May Cottage. Of course Lou didn't blame her, but she did miss Robin's regular visits to the farm.

Rob apologised for his absence. 'But Mum says she needs me at home, Auntie Lou.'

'You don't have to apologise, Rob.

Marina's your mum. Of course she wants you with her. She loves you.'

'And I love her too, but I want to see you as well.'

'I'm always here when you need me. You know that.'

But it wasn't only Rob who Lou missed. She missed Wes, too.

She saw him whizzing by in his silver Porsche, but he was never at the supermarket or post office or school. Marina dealt with all the day-to-day things. It was almost as if Wes had been transported to another planet, except when she saw him with Marina at the various festive functions in the village.

To increase her misery, Wes and Marina made the ideal couple; both of them tall, fair and elegant.

Lou realised that she had never really stood a chance.

* * *

Lou went through the motions of preparing for Christmas. There was always so much to do and usually she enjoyed the hustle and bustle. But this year her heart wasn't in it. Instead, she felt lonely and sad. It was like grieving all over again, but this time for someone living. Someone whom she saw arm-in-arm with another woman.

She wrestled with the Christmas tree, decorating it lavishly to make up for her own inner bleakness. She wrote the greetings cards and wrapped all the stocking fillers and boys' gifts, leaving one for Rob on the doorstep of the cottage when she was sure both Marina and Wes were out.

She cleaned the house from top to bottom, sorted out all the boys' clothes and cooked and cooked and cooked until she was exhausted.

On Christmas Eve she was lying down by the open fire in the lounge, waiting for the boys to go to sleep. There was lots of giggling and whispering going on upstairs.

The boys were full of excitement.

Not only was Santa Claus on his way, but it as going to be a white Christmas too.

The snow had been falling for a couple of days. Lou had spent the afternoon on the slopes, sledging with the boys, and now she was so tired and stiff she could barely move.

She'd had a long hot soak in the bath and was now snuggled in her fleecy blue PJs, plaid gown and red thick woolly socks. She stuck her aching legs up on the couch to get the blood circulating and lay there, willing the boys to go to sleep so she could stuff their stockings before crawling into bed herself.

She was so tired that she dozed off. A while later she was woken with a start by the dog barking.

'Quiet, Ollie,' she hissed. 'You'll wake the boys.'

Then she heard the back door latch rattle. Was it her imagination or had someone entered the kitchen?

Concerned, Lou propped herself up

on her elbows. 'Who's there?' Next she heard the chink of glasses being taken out of the cupboard. 'Luke? Dan?'

'No, it's me.' Wes stood there with snow freckled in his hair and on his dark jacket. He was holding a bottle of champagne in one hand and glasses in the other.

'Wes!' she squeaked in surprise.

'May I join you?'

'Well . . . ' She tugged her dressing gown tighter around her. 'I'm not dressed for visitors.' And especially not this one!

'You look beautiful to me.'

'Beautiful? Have you been drinking too much wine at Midnight Mass?'

Wes chuckled as he took off his jacket and slung it over a chair. He then hunkered down next to her.

'Champagne?' he said.

'Well . . . ' She nervously tucked a curl behind her ear. Another sprang out and took its place.

Wes popped the cork and poured the frothy liquid into the two glasses.

159

'Are Marina and Rob with you?' She glanced towards the door.

'Nope. Cheers.' He clinked the glasses together and than handed one to her.

9

Lou, still propped up on her elbows, took it and dubiously stared down at the sparkling champagne. Her heart was thumping hard in her chest. Her throat felt tight and constricted. Why was he here? And why was he alone? And what was with the champers?

'Is everything OK?' she asked hesitantly.

'Yup.'

'I see.' But she didn't. She took a sip of bubbles exploded at the back of her throat. She coughed and put the glass on the hearth.

Wes cocked his head to one side, 'Any reason why you're lying on the floor?'

'I've been sledging all afternoon with the boys.'

'Say no more. I'll join you.' With that Wes lay next to her, which made Lou feel even more hot and uncomfortable. What did he want? She shuffled closer to the hearth and away from his long, hard body.

'Nice socks,' he said.

'Thank you.'

'An improvement on the pink fluffy slippers.'

'There's nothing wrong with my slippers.'

'And I'm getting used to the dressing gown.'

She didn't deign to reply.

'Did you know that you've got stains on your ceiling?' he added conversationally.

'OK. That's it. If you're here to make personal comments, you can leave.'

'Sorry.' He didn't budge. 'I didn't mean to be rude.'

Lou could swear he was smiling but as she was flat on her back and staring at that same wretched stained ceiling she couldn't sneak a look.

'I could paint it for you.'

'Go!'

'It wouldn't take long.'

'Wes, the state of the ceiling doesn't concern me tonight. So shut up and go home. You've got a family to go to and I've got stockings to fill.'

'I don't.'

'Well, Rob's a bit old to have a stocking I suppose.' Though she'd got one for Luke.

'No, I meant I don't have a family to go back to.'

Lou's heart lurched. 'What do you mean?' She turned on her side and propped herself on an elbow. Wes remained staring at the ceiling.

'Marina has taken Rob to France for the holidays.'

'Why didn't you go too?'

'I didn't want to.'

'Oh Wes, you've got to try harder if you want to make your marriage work.'

He suddenly turned towards her.

'I did try, dammit. I tried for Rob, but I'm not the man Marina wants. She's in love with someone else. She only came back because she felt guilty about Rob. And because she wanted some more money.' He sounded bitter.

'I'm so sorry, Wes.'

'I'm not. I stopped loving her a long time ago. This isn't the first time she's fallen in love with someone else or that she's run out of money. And it won't be the last. But now we're divorced, it doesn't affect me so much. We've sorted out our differences and, more importantly, Rob understands. We can all move on.'

'I thought you two were the perfect couple. You seemed so well matched.'

'Looks are deceiving. We were living a lie. I don't want to live like that anymore. I've already wasted too much time.'

Wes reached for one of Lou's curls and tugged it slightly.

Lou blushed.

'I'm sorry for the past few weeks. It's been so hard staying away from you. But I wanted to sort things out with Marina without dragging you into the fray. But believe me, my heart's been here all the time.'

Lou blushed harder, unable to speak.

'You know,' carried on Wes. 'That I've come to the conclusion that the whole village loves Aunt Lou. And I'm at the top of the list.'

'You're being silly,' she managed to squeak.

'It's true. Henry's always singing your praises.'

'Well Henry's a sweetie.'

'I wouldn't quite describe him like that! But I'm not here to discuss Henry's attributes.'

'Why are you here?'

'To see how you feel about being the mother to seven or eight boys?' Wes asked.

'Seven or eight boys?'

'You said you wanted a baby or two.'

'Yes, but that makes it six or seven, not eight. Honestly, for a businessman your maths sucks.' She took a swig of champagne.

'But if you marry me, then you'll be step-mum to Rob too.'

'Marry you?' Bubbles went up her nose and hit the throat again. Her eyes watered and she began to splutter.

'Yes, marry me and I'll make your dream come true.'

Lou did a fish impersonation.

'And,' Wes continued. 'You'll make mine come true too. Merry Christmas, Aunt Lou!' And then he kissed her.

THE END

We do hope that you have enjoyed reading this large print book.

Did you know that all of our titles are available for purchase?

We publish a wide range of high quality large print books including:
Romances, Mysteries, Classics
General Fiction
Non Fiction and Westerns

Special interest titles available in large print are:
The Little Oxford Dictionary
Music Book, Song Book
Hymn Book, Service Book

Also available from us courtesy of Oxford University Press:
Young Readers' Dictionary
(large print edition)
Young Readers' Thesaurus
(large print edition)

For further information or a free brochure, please contact us at:
Ulverscroft Large Print Books Ltd.,
The Green, Bradgate Road, Anstey,
Leicester, LE7 7FU, England.
Tel: (00 44) **0116 236 4325**
Fax: (00 44) **0116 234 0205**

Other titles in the
Linford Romance Library:

AN IMAGE OF YOU

Liz Fielding

Millionaire Sir Charles Bainbridge, at the end of his patience with his daughter Georgette's behaviour, sends her to Kenya. Humiliatingly, she must work as an assistant to the ultimate male chauvinist Lukas on a location shoot. They met once before . . . in rather strained circumstances! In fact, she'd showered him with flour and he hadn't been pleased. And now she must be nice to him. This will take every ounce of acting ability Georgette possesses — and she is no actress.

TO LOVE AGAIN

Jasmina Svenne

After a disastrous romance in her youth, Juliet Radley has given up hope of marriage and become reconciled to a quiet life as Amy Gibson's governess. However, despite her expectations, she grows attached to Captain Richard Gibson, her employer's cousin — the only house guest to treat her with consideration. But a new arrival threatens her happiness: the rakish Hugh Faversham is the one man in the world who can expose her darkest secret . . .

DISTANT SUN

Sheila Holroyd

When, unexpectedly, a free cruise down the Nile is offered to Cathy she thinks it's the answer to her holiday problems. All she has to do is see if there is any way of improving the experience . . . Instead, she finds herself in danger from unknown enemies who will stop at nothing to get what they want. How can she tell friend from foe? Who can she trust? And romance with a charming stranger makes Cathy's life even more complicated . . .